BONE CHILLING!

Frank and Gwen froze, their hearts pounding, as a black-suited diver raised a speargun and pointed it directly at them.

Frank and Gwen didn't want to startle the other diver, knowing that any mistake might get them killed.

The diver also seemed unsure of what to do. Still pointing the speargun, he backed toward the exit. But he wasn't looking where he was going. Without realizing it, he was about to back into the skeleton.

The skeleton seemed to reach out to embrace the diver as he bumped into it. A bony hand floated in front of his mask.

The diver jerked his arm wildly up to free himself. In his panic, he squeezed the trigger—and sent a deadly spear right at Frank!

Books in THE HARDY BOYS CASEFILES™ Series

Available from ARCHWAY Paperbacks

DEAD IN THE WATER

FRANKLIN W. DIXON

AN ARCHWAY PAPERBACK
Published by POCKET BOOKS
New York London Toronto Sydney Tokyo Singapore

AN ARCHWAY PAPERBACK *Original*

An Archway Paperback published by
POCKET BOOKS, a division of Simon & Schuster Inc.
1230 Avenue of the Americas, New York, NY 10020

Copyright © 1998 by Simon & Schuster Inc.
Produced by Mega-Books, Inc.

ISBN: 0-671-56242-8

First Archway Paperback printing January 1998

10 9 8 7 6 5 4 3 2 1

THE HARDY BOYS, AN ARCHWAY PAPERBACK
and colophon are registered trademarks of Simon & Schuster Inc.

THE HARDY BOYS CASEFILES is a trademark
of Simon & Schuster Inc.

Cover art by John Youssi

Printed in the U.S.A.

IL 6+

Chapter

1

JOE HARDY HAD A CHILLING THOUGHT as he stared out the airplane window at the Florida coastline. "If a submarine sank back in World War II, would the wreck still be full of skeletons?" he wondered out loud.

Next to him, his brother, Frank, looked up from the scuba-diving magazine he was reading. "It's hard to say," he answered. "In the tropics, where the water is warm, a skeleton would decompose pretty quickly. But in deep, cold water, I guess it could last for fifty years or so."

Joe had seen a lot of adventure in his seventeen years, but the thought of finding a human skeleton in the belly of a sunken submarine raised the hair on the back of his neck.

1

He'd always wanted to go wreck-diving. He'd been scuba diving before, in the Bahamas, when he and Frank had helped find the treasure from the *Doña Bonita*, a Spanish galleon. But that ship had crumbled into sand hundreds of years ago, so only the treasure had remained. He hadn't been able to explore the wreck itself.

"From what I've heard, it would be dark and cramped inside a submarine wreck," Joe said, shifting his six-foot frame in the tiny airplane seat. "The wreck would be full of muck and silt that would make it easy to get lost. It would be dangerous, but who knows what you'd find? It would be worth the risk."

"We're not here to go scuba diving," Frank reminded him. "We're here to help Dad's friend Alvin Mann."

A year older and an inch taller than Joe, Frank shared his brother's thirst for adventure, but he was more likely to think before leaping, rather than the other way around.

All the same, Frank was just as anxious as Joe to touch down in Florida. The sooner they got off the plane, the sooner they'd find out what the mysterious phone call they'd gotten two days earlier was all about—the call that had brought them to Florida.

Frank thought back to the moment the call had come. It had been Monday evening, just before five. They had been about to take their father, Detective Fenton Hardy, to the airport, and had been running late. Mr. Hardy had put the call on the speakerphone so that Frank and Joe could listen in.

The caller was Alvin Mann, an old friend of Mr. Hardy's who ran a marine salvage business in St. Augustine, Florida.

"This is the real thing," Mann's voice had boomed over the speaker. "I've been looking for this submarine since the Second World War. Now I've found it, but I need your help."

"Of course I'll help," Fenton Hardy had answered. "Unfortunately, I'm about to catch a plane. Can I call you in a few hours?"

"I'll have to call you," Mann answered, his voice urgent. "I don't have a phone in my trailer. And don't try to call me at the business, either, because there's been trouble with my partner. If you could come down here, that would be best. I know it's short notice, but I'll make it worth your while. We'll be rich."

"I'm afraid that's out of the question," Fenton said. "I just took on an important case and I'm going to be out of touch for about ten days." He looked at his watch. "In fact, I can't talk now. It's almost five o'clock. I need to get to the airport."

"Five o'clock!" Mann exclaimed. "I didn't realize how late it was. I've got to get to the post office before it closes. I'll call you back in an hour."

"But I won't be here," Fenton began, but Mann had hung up before he could finish.

On the way to the airport, Fenton had told his sons, "You'll have to talk to Mann when he calls back. Use your judgment, and help him as best you can."

"We'll be glad to go down there," Joe had said. "I thought these last few days of vacation were going to be a waste. Didn't Mann say we could become rich?"

"Be careful," Fenton had warned. "Treasure hunting is Mann's passion, but it's a dangerous game. It's cost him a lot—including his family, who left him years ago because of it."

Frank and Joe had waited all the next day for another call from Mann, but it hadn't come. They had tried directory assistance, but there was no listing for an Alvin Mann. Finally, on a hunch, Joe had called the St. Augustine police, and had learned that Mann's granddaughter had reported him missing.

After that there had been no holding them back. "Dad would want us to go down there," Joe had insisted, and their mother had finally agreed. They had booked tickets on the next possible flight to St. Augustine.

A uniformed stewardess approached, bringing Frank back to the present. "We'll be landing in a few minutes. Please return your seat back to the full upright position."

Frank straightened his seat, then leaned over his brother to look out the window. He could see the town ahead, surrounded by the glistening waters of Matanzas Bay.

"I'm looking forward to seeing the town," he said. "St. Augustine is the oldest European settlement in North America. This place was a major port for the treasure fleets that sailed in those days. Billions of dollars worth of gold and silver must have come through here."

The popping in their ears told the Hardys they were descending, and a few minutes later they felt the thump of the wheels as the plane touched down and taxied to the terminal.

"Please remove all carry-on bags as you deplane through the jetway," the stewardess said over the loudspeaker as Frank and Joe walked off the plane.

Half an hour later they had claimed their bags and were exiting the terminal. The sky was overcast, and the air was still damp from a recent rain.

Joe wiped his brow, already beginning to feel the humidity. "Okay, so what's our plan?" he asked.

"Mom gave me Mann's business card. She found it in Dad's desk," Frank answered. He pulled a tattered card out of his wallet. " 'Mann and Payne Marine,'" he read aloud. "I think we should go over there and see what we find."

"Mann said there had been trouble with his partner," Joe pointed out.

"Trouble is why we're here," Frank answered. "We'll have to get mixed up in it sooner or later."

From the airport, a short cab-ride down U.S. Route 1 brought them into town, where the highway turned into Ponce de Leon Boulevard. On their right was a long, narrow bay. The left side of the road was lined with shops and businesses.

The cab driver turned left onto a narrow road, drove to the end, and stopped at a large marina. Frank noticed that the sign out front read Branson Marine. Even more noticeable, however, were several police cars parked outside, lights flashing.

"You're sure this is the right address?" Frank asked.

The driver nodded. "Number Five Boatyard Road."

Not sure what else to do, Frank and Joe paid the driver and walked toward the showroom, still carrying their bags. Outside, a policeman leaned on his squad car, speaking into a radio. Inside, several policemen were talking to a dark-haired man and a tall teenager with baggy shorts and shaggy, blond hair. Nobody seemed to notice the Hardys as they walked in.

"He robbed me," the dark-haired man was saying, his face red with anger. He was about fifty, with well-combed hair that somehow matched his sharp nose and tight navy blue knit shirt.

"Now, Ted, you don't know that," one of the policemen said, a square-jawed man with a high forehead. "Let's get all the facts before we start accusing people."

"I know the facts!" the man insisted. "I want him found, and I want him prosecuted."

"Don't tell me how to do my job," the policeman replied, an edge in his voice. "We'll handle it. We've had an all-points bulletin out on him since yesterday, when his granddaughter reported him missing. If he's anywhere to be found, we'll find him."

Branson clapped his hand on his forehead. "He's missing," he muttered. "That makes it even more obvious that he's guilty."

The blond-haired guy tried to speak up for the first time. "Dad, maybe we should—"

"Dennis, shut up!" the man snapped. Then he noticed the Hardys. He turned and glared at them. "What do you want?"

"Sorry to interrupt," Joe began, taken off guard. "We must have the wrong address or something. We were looking for Alvin Mann. We thought this was his business."

"*His* business!" the red-faced man snapped. "That's a laugh. It's *my* business now, and has been for over a year. I'm Ted Branson."

The square-jawed policeman folded his arms across his chest and looked at the Hardys. "Who are you?" he asked.

"Friends of Mann's, visiting from out of town," Joe answered.

"What's going on here?" Frank asked.

"I'll ask the questions," the policeman said. "But, for your information, Alvin Mann is a fugitive from the law at the moment."

"A fugitive," Branson sneered. "That's a nice way to put it. Mann is a thief. He robbed me of thousands of dollars' worth of equipment."

Chapter

2

"MANN CAME HERE the day before yesterday, wanting to borrow several thousand dollars' worth of equipment for some crazy salvage scheme," Branson explained. "I told him no, and today my equipment is missing. Who else knew how to get into the storeroom? It's robbery, plain and simple."

"Now, Ted, calm down," the policeman said. "Mann used to be your partner. If he did take the equipment, I'm sure he plans to return it."

"It's too late for that," Branson snarled. He looked at Frank and Joe again. "Where did you two come from, and why, of all days, are you looking for Mann now?"

"We're friends from out of town," Frank answered. "We flew in this afternoon to help with a project he's working on."

"What project was that?" the policeman asked.

"A marine salvage project," Frank said. "He didn't tell us much about it."

"You're mighty good friends, flying down here without even knowing what for," Branson said.

Frank met his gaze evenly. "Our father has known Mann for a long time," he said.

"Everybody calm down," the policeman said, pulling out a notebook. "Let's start from the beginning. I'll need statements from everybody—including you two," he added, looking at Frank and Joe.

More than an hour later, Frank and Joe finally left the marina. The policeman, Sergeant Sauter, had questioned them at length. The sergeant had given them a number to call if they had any more information on Mann, and had advised them to return home to Bayport.

"Talk about a cross-examination," Joe said after they had left the marina and were walking back toward the main road, still carrying the bags they had brought from Bayport. "I thought we'd never get out of there. But I can't believe Dad's friend could possibly be a thief."

"Neither do I," Frank answered. "I think Sergeant Sauter could be right that he borrowed the equipment, planning to return it. But if he did it without permission, then, technically, it's stealing."

"Branson sure has it in for Mann," Joe said. "I wonder what happened between them."

"I have an idea how we might find out," Frank answered. He walked toward a small bait shop several buildings down from the marina. A woman watched them from the doorway as they approached.

"Good afternoon," Frank greeted the woman. "There's been lots of excitement down at the marina this afternoon."

"What's it all about?" the woman asked. "I've seen police cars coming and going all afternoon."

"Some equipment is missing, and Mr. Branson thinks it might have been stolen," Joe answered.

"Hmm," the woman said. "Seems to me he could afford to lose a thing or two. He's got plenty of money. He only joined that business three years ago, and now he owns the whole thing."

"Didn't Alvin Mann use to be one of the owners?" Frank asked.

The woman nodded, then smiled. "I knew Alvin Mann well. Crusty old guy, but I liked him. He used to stop by to complain about one thing or another. Either the weather was bad, the fish weren't biting, business was slow." She shook her head. "Of course, that was before the accident."

"What accident?" Frank asked.

"It happened over a year ago," she said. "Alvin was diving with Dennis Branson—that's Ted Branson's son—and Dennis stayed down too long and got the bends—you know, what divers get sometimes?"

Frank nodded. As an experienced diver, he was familiar with the bends, also called decompression sickness. The condition was caused by nitrogen bubbles that formed in the blood when a diver surfaced too quickly after an especially long or deep dive.

"Dennis could have died," the woman continued. "Ted Branson blamed Alvin for what happened, and ran him out of the business. It was a shame, especially since Alvin was the one who started the business."

"Do you know where we can find Mann now?" Frank asked.

She nodded. "He lives in a trailer north of Vilano Beach. Take State Road A1A north to Conch Road. Turn left and drive to the end. Keep going and you'll see the trailer off in the trees."

"Never underestimate the power of gossip," Frank said as they continued toward the main road to find a cab.

Vilano Beach was located across the bay from St. Augustine. Apparently Conch Road was fairly remote, because Frank and Joe had to ask several cab drivers before one agreed to take them there.

As they drove through town, the driver pointed out the sights. "On your right is the Castillo de San Marcos, the old fort," he said. "For hundreds of years that fort protected the town from invasion. The entire population of St. Augustine would crowd inside for weeks or months at a time."

Frank looked at the low stone structure, amazed that something so small could have had such military significance. The walls were barely thirty feet high. A single modern bomber could have leveled the whole place in minutes, he figured.

After crossing the bridge to Vilano Beach, the cab continued north up the coast for about ten minutes before turning left in front of a small motel.

"Here we are—Conch Road," the driver announced. He drove another mile or so until the paved road ended. "Looks like this is as far as we go," he said.

A narrow dirt road continued into the trees, but a parked police car blocked them from going any farther. A policeman climbed out of the squad car and walked up to the taxi as it

13

approached. "I have to ask you to turn your vehicle around," he instructed them.

Joe rolled down the window. "We're looking for Alvin Mann. He lives down this road."

"Are you a relative of Mann's?"

"A friend," Joe answered.

"Then all I can tell you is that Mann isn't home," the policeman said. "Now, I have to ask you again to turn your vehicle around," he repeated.

"Sorry you guys had to come out here for nothing," the driver said as he maneuvered the cab around. "I still have to charge you for the ride out, but the trip back to town is on me."

"Thanks for the offer, but how about dropping us at that motel we saw on our way in?" Frank suggested.

The cabbie shrugged. "Suit yourself."

A minute later they pulled up in front of the Conch Motel and Cafe. The vacancy sign was lit. Joe surveyed the parking lot. It was empty, except for a single car.

"Frank, maybe something closer to town would be a bit livelier," he said after they had gotten out of the cab.

"Hey, little bro," Frank said. "We're not here to party. I think we should stay near Mann's trailer. If we sneak back after dark, maybe we can find some clue as to what happened to him."

14

After checking in, they sat down for a quick dinner at the cafe next door to the motel. From their table they could see the road through the window. Joe was almost finished eating when a police car drove past, coming from the road that led to Mann's trailer. "There goes our friend," he said. "Time to move."

The air was warm and damp as they started out. Despite the heat, they both wore long-sleeved shirts and dark pants to make themselves harder to see.

"What a lovely, cool evening," Joe joked, wiping the sweat from his brow. "It's just as muggy now as it was during the day."

"I think I just felt a raindrop," Frank answered. "That should cool you down."

"Great," Joe muttered. Soon they were walking through a driving rain. They had almost reached the point where the policeman had turned them back when they heard a car approaching behind them.

"Let's get off the road," Frank said. "I don't want to be seen."

"That wasn't a police car," Joe said after the car had driven past. "That was a pickup truck."

"I wonder what it's doing heading for Mann's trailer," Frank said.

"You got me," Joe said as they continued on, staying off the road to avoid being seen. Passing the point where the police car had turned them

15

back, they followed the dirt road into the woods.

Leading the way, Frank saw a light blink in the trees ahead. He wiped a raindrop from his eye and looked again. "Did you see that light?" he asked.

"No," Joe said, behind Frank. "Too much rain."

A few minutes later a trailer came into view. The windows were dark, Joe noticed. In the gloomy night, he thought the trailer had a forlorn, abandoned look, surrounded as it was by bushes and low trees.

Mann must have liked his privacy, Joe thought, to live out here in these lonely woods without even a telephone.

Frank pulled out a flashlight and shone it on the trailer. The name Mann was painted on a wooden sign above the door. "At least we know we're in the right place," he said.

Frank knocked several times on the door— just in case someone was inside—but there was no answer. Frank wrestled through the bushes to reach a front window. He stood on his toes and shone his light inside, straining to see past the curtains. Was that a movement he saw in the darkness, he wondered, or—

A stick cracked behind him, so close it made him whirl around. "Joe, is that you?"

"Back here." His brother's voice came from behind the trailer. "Take a look at this."

Frank walked around the trailer, following his brother's voice. A yellow Jeep was parked among the trees. Joe took the flashlight and peered inside. "This thing's loaded," he said admiringly. "Four-liter engine, alloy wheels, CD player, plus a holder for a cellular phone."

"Not exactly the car I'd expect Mann to drive," Frank said, pushing aside a branch to look at the front fender. "It even has custom license plates. What do you suppose NEES-TER means?"

Before Joe could answer, a loud crash came from inside the trailer. They ran back to the front and pounded several times on the door. "Mr. Mann?" Frank called. "Are you in there?"

"I say we force the door," Joe said.

Frank kneeled and looked at the lock. "This shouldn't be too tough," he said, pulling a knife-like utensil from his pocket. "If you can push the door in a bit, I should be able to slide this into the crack."

Joe strained against the door as Frank worked the lock. "One more second and I should be able to trip the mechanism," Frank said.

Joe was still leaning hard against the door when it flew open. He tumbled into the trailer, landing on his hands and knees.

He stood up quickly, groping back toward the

door as he struggled to find his balance in the darkness. He had a strange feeling he wasn't alone in the trailer.

"Frank, hand me that flashlight!" he called.

"Here you go," he heard Frank answer. Joe turned toward his brother's voice, and for an instant was blinded by the beam of the flashlight shining at him.

Then he heard his brother grunt and the light dropped to the floor.

"Frank!" Joe called. He heard the door slam shut and somebody moved toward him. The flashlight glimmered where it lay. He could make out the silhouette of a figure standing next to the door. "Is that you?" he asked.

Joe waited only a second for an answer that didn't come, then lowered his head and charged forward.

The silhouette darted neatly out of his path. Before Joe could adjust his direction, pain ripped through the back of his neck. He reeled forward and fell to the ground, struggling to stay conscious as his attacker landed heavily on him, pinning him in a choke hold.

Chapter

3

"JOE!" FRANK GASPED FOR BREATH. Something had hit him in the stomach as he'd stepped into the dark trailer, knocking him outside again and taking the wind out of him. He'd dropped the flashlight inside the trailer. The door had slammed in front of him, trapping Joe inside.

Frank jumped to his feet and tugged on the doorknob, but it was locked again. Inside, he thought he heard his brother groan, then fall to the floor.

He pounded on the door with his fist. "Joe!" he shouted. Stepping back, he lunged against the door with all his weight. This time the lock gave with a crashing sound as the door flew open.

Frank tumbled into the trailer and immediately tripped over a body. His flashlight lay where he had dropped it, casting a sliver of light across the floor. He could make out Joe wrestling with somebody. Reaching forward, Frank grabbed his brother's attacker in a headlock, trying to pull the assailant off.

"Let go of me, you jerk!" It was a female voice.

Frank was so startled that he released his grip and stepped back. He picked up the flashlight and shone it on the scene in front of him.

Joe lay on the floor, half pinning—and half pinned by—a slender young woman. As Frank stood watching, she thumped her fists on Joe's muscular arm. "Let go of me!" she repeated, yelling in his ear. Still groggy, Joe obeyed.

The young woman scrambled away from Joe, tripping over a chair as she struggled to find her feet. Snapping on a light, she ran to the kitchen, grabbed a large chef's knife, and held it in front of her.

"You'd better get out of here," she said, a mix of anger and fear in her voice. "I called the police when I heard you drive up. They should be here any minute."

"Easy," Frank said, his eyes glued on the knife. "We don't mean any harm." He shot a quick glance toward his brother. "Joe, are you all right?"

Joe nodded. Frank noticed that his brother looked groggy, but he was sitting upright.

"The police are on their way," the young woman repeated. Frank guessed she was a few years older than he, probably in her early twenties. She had long brown hair and brown eyes.

"We're looking for Alvin Mann," Frank said. "We're Frank and Joe Hardy, old friends."

The young woman scowled. "Do you always break into people's homes if they don't answer the door?"

"When we heard that crash, we thought Mr. Mann might be in trouble," Frank answered.

Joe stood up, rubbing his neck. "We also didn't know whose Jeep was parked out back, or what—"

"You didn't break into that, too, did you?" the woman snapped, interrupting him.

"Relax," Joe answered. "Your Jeep is fine. I wish I could say the same about my neck. What did you hit me with?"

"A diver's weight belt." She indicated a belt that lay on the floor. "Lucky for you it's a modern belt, made of rubber. They used to make the weights out of lead."

"Lucky for me," Joe said with the hint of a smile.

"Who are you?" Frank asked.

"I'm Alvin Mann's granddaughter, Anita."

"Why didn't you answer the door when we knocked?" Joe asked.

"Pardon me for not being more sociable." Anita snorted. "You guys drive up in the middle of the night, peek in the windows, then pound down the door. What do you expect me to do—offer you dinner?"

"It's hardly the middle of the night," Joe said.

"And we didn't drive up, we walked," Frank said.

"I heard a car," Anita insisted.

"Then there's somebody else around here," Frank said, walking to the door and looking out.

"I'm not worried about who's out there," Anita said. "I'm worried about who's in here."

"If we were here to hurt you, we would have done so by now," Joe said gently. "Your grandfather called our dad two nights ago. Our dad had to go away on business. That's why we came."

"What time did he call?" Anita asked.

Joe thought a moment. "Around five, I guess."

"He called me right after that," Anita said quickly. "He was very excited. He told me that he'd hit the jackpot, and we'd be rich. Before he could explain, he was cut off in the middle of a sentence. I heard him groan. Then the connection went dead."

Concern grew on Anita's face as she continued. "I knew right then that something had happened to him. I waited for him to call back, but he didn't. Finally, I called the police. They traced the number to a pay phone in town.

"The police said they'd handle it, but I couldn't sleep. I called Ted Branson, his former partner, but he hung up on me. I also tried to reach Burt Sculley, his first mate. Finally I got into my Jeep and drove here in the middle of the night. I live in Jacksonville, about an hour away."

As Anita spoke, Joe found himself admiring her courage. She'd come here out of concern for her grandfather, ignoring her own safety. "You should be more careful," he said. "There's no telling what you might have found here."

Anita threw him a quick smile, then went on. "I looked all over town but couldn't find him anywhere. Finally, I found his car parked at the dock where he moors his boat, not far from here. His boat is gone . . ." Her voice trailed off.

"You realize that the police are looking for your grandfather as a possible robbery suspect," Frank said.

Anita's eyes blazed. "I know. That's ridiculous."

"Could he have borrowed the equipment?" Joe asked. "When he called us, he said something about finding a World War II submarine."

Anita sat down on the couch and sighed. "Grandpa's lifelong obsession is to find the wreck of U-317, a German sub that sank off St. Augustine in 1944.

"He was a sailor in the Coast Guard during the war, and his ship picked up the only survivor from the submarine," she explained. "Grandpa spoke some German, so he was put in charge of the survivor, a seaman named Klaus Krueger. Krueger didn't live long. Before he died, though, he told my grandfather that the submarine was carrying millions in gold when it went down."

The rain picked up outside, pattering loudly on the roof. Frank and Joe exchanged a long glance, waiting for Anita to go on.

"U-317 became an obsession," she continued. "He risked his business, his family, even his life. His partners were caught up in it, too."

"You mean Ted Branson?" Joe asked.

She nodded. "Also his original partner, Waldo Payne, and Branson's son, Dennis. They all became obsessed, until Dennis almost died in an accident last year."

"We heard about that," Frank said.

"The accident wasn't my grandfather's fault," Anita said vehemently. "Everyone knew Dennis was a reckless diver. If anyone was responsible, it was Ted Branson himself. He's the one who constantly rode his son. Dennis would have done anything to please his father."

"Let's suppose your grandfather found the

submarine," Joe said. "He'd need help salvaging it. So maybe he went to Branson for help and got turned down. Maybe that's when he called us. He also called you, but the call was interrupted."

"It's obvious what happened," Anita said. "Branson has had it in for my grandfather ever since the accident, maybe even longer. Now he has a clear motive to get rid of my grandfather—either by framing him, or doing something worse—so he can keep the gold for himself."

"Branson wouldn't be the only suspect," Frank pointed out. "Anybody who knew Krueger's story about the gold would be a possibility. That would include Waldo Payne and Dennis Branson. Anybody else?"

"Payne isn't a suspect," Anita said. "He and Grandpa have been friends since the war. They were sailors together. Maybe Burt Sculley, Grandpa's current first mate. Other than them, I don't think he told anybody. He was very secretive about it. He didn't want anybody else to find the sub before he did."

Frank looked out the door again. "Did you guys hear anything just now?" he asked.

"I've been hearing things all day," Anita answered. "My imagination is probably running wild, but I think that whoever went after my grandfather might be after me. This morning I called a friend in Jacksonville who went to my house to feed my dog. She said a car was parked out front, with two men in it."

"If you think somebody is after you, this trailer isn't a very safe place," Frank said, thinking about the pickup truck that had passed them on the road, and the noises he had heard.

Anita nodded. "I'm ready to get out of here. I only came to get my grandfather's journal, but I can't find it anywhere. Usually he keeps it on his desk. Normally I wouldn't think of reading it, but I thought it might give a clue as to what happened to him."

"You said before the police were coming," Joe pointed out. "Should we wait until they get here?"

"Oh, yeah," Anita answered. "But we can at least warm up the Jeep."

Leaving the trailer, they walked around to the spot where the Jeep was parked in back. Even in the darkness, Frank and Joe could tell immediately that something was wrong. The Jeep sat too low on its wheels.

Anita gasped. "My tires!"

"They've been slashed," Frank said grimly.

"How will we get out of here?" Anita asked, fear returning to her voice.

"We'll just go the way Joe and I came—on foot. Shouldn't the police be here soon, though?" Frank asked.

"They aren't really coming." Anita moaned. She looked wildly into the trees around her. "I only told you that to scare you away."

"So, call the police now," Joe said, puzzled. "We know your grandfather doesn't have a phone, but I saw a holder for a cell phone in your Jeep."

Anita shook her head. "When I left Jacksonville, I was in such a hurry I forgot to bring it."

After Anita grabbed a few of her things and stuffed them into a small backpack, the three started out. The rain had died down, but it was now completely dark, with clouds blocking out the moon.

Frank and Joe could see that Anita was close to panic. Joe asked her questions to keep her mind occupied. "What does 'Neester' mean?" he wanted to know, referring to her custom license plate.

"That's the name of my company, Neester Productions," she answered. "I produce TV commercials. It comes from an old nickname."

"I hear a car approaching," Frank interrupted. "Let's get off the road."

A pickup truck rolled into sight, moving slowly, its engine rattling. Frank couldn't tell if it was the same truck they had seen before.

Anita jumped up. "That's my grandfather's truck!"

"Wait!" Joe called, but it was too late. Anita

had already run out into the road. As she ran into the glare of the headlights, the truck stopped and the driver climbed out.

Frank and Joe were on their feet. "Grandpa?" they heard Anita shout. The door opened on the passenger side of the truck, and Anita took a step back.

Joe ran toward her at full speed. "Anita! Get out of the road!" Anita must have heard him, because she took another step back.

The two men jumped back into the truck and shut the doors. The truck began to move forward. Anita turned and began to run, but slipped on the wet, sandy ground.

Then the wheels squealed as the driver punched the accelerator. Joe watched in horror as the truck hurtled straight for Anita!

Chapter

4

"ANITA!" JOE RAN TOWARD HER at full speed, straight into the path of the truck. He had only a moment to act. If he made a headlong dive, he might be able to knock Anita out of the way in time. He didn't have time to worry about how he'd get himself out of the way.

Time seemed to move in slow motion as the truck covered the last few feet. One more step and Joe would make his fatal leap.

Miraculously, the truck veered to one side and careened harmlessly around Anita, missing her by inches.

Frank, Joe, and Anita watched, astonished, as the truck drove a hundred feet down the road, screeched to a stop, turned, and came back toward them at full speed. This time they easily jumped out of the way as the truck sped past and disappeared in the direction it had come from.

"I thought I was going to die," Anita gasped, hugging her arms tightly around her. "I know it was stupid for me to run into the road, but I was positive it was my grandfather's truck."

"Whoever was driving was sure surprised to see anyone out here on the road," Joe said. "Since there's no one out this way, they had to be going to your grandfather's place."

"So, the question is, who were they and what did they want?" Frank said.

"And when will they be back?" Anita added. "I'm not sure I want the answer to that one."

It was a long, nerve-racking walk back to the Conch Motel. They stayed near the edge of the road the whole way, ready to run into the woods if the truck appeared again. Frank and Joe tried to make conversation along the way to keep the mood light, and when the Conch Motel finally came into view, all three breathed a sigh of relief.

The clock showed five minutes before midnight as they walked into the motel office. Nobody was at the desk, but Anita rang the bell and a moment later a clerk appeared. As soon as he gave her a key, she grabbed her bag and started down the hall.

"Good night, guys," she told them. "I can't say it's been fun, but things could have turned out a lot worse if you hadn't showed up."

"What a day," Joe said as soon as he and Frank were settled in their own room. "What a girl," he added under his breath.

Frank overheard him and guessed his brother's thoughts. "She has a lot of courage," he said as he switched off the light, "but isn't she a little bit old for you? And what about Vanessa?"

Joe didn't respond to Frank's question about Vanessa, the girl he dated back home in Bayport. Instead he lay awake in the dark, thinking about Anita. She did have a lot of courage—and something else, too, he thought. He fell asleep picturing her warm eyes and long brown hair.

The next morning Frank and Joe woke up early and knocked on the door of Anita's room. They had to knock several times before she answered, rubbing her eyes. She looked as if she hadn't slept well.

After calling a mechanic to go fix the tires on the Jeep, they sat down in the cafe next to the motel for a quick breakfast while they waited for the tow truck to show up.

Twenty-five minutes later a large flatbed truck pulled up in front of the motel. The driver opened the door for them, a bald-headed man with the name Tex written on his shirt.

The police car had returned to its position at the entrance to Mann's driveway. Sitting in the cab of the truck, Frank and Joe recognized the police officer they had met in the same spot the day before.

"Like I told you guys yesterday, Mann isn't around," the policeman said. "This is private property, so I'll have to ask you to come back another time."

Leaning over Frank and Joe, Anita stuck her head out the window. "I'm Alvin Mann's granddaughter," she announced. "I have permission to use his trailer whenever I want."

The policeman started to object, but Anita held up her hand. "Where were you last night when somebody slashed the tires on my Jeep? We had to walk back to the highway and nearly got run down by a pickup truck. Maybe if you weren't so busy trying to arrest my grandfather, you'd have noticed.

"Now, if you don't mind, I'd like to get my Jeep," Anita continued. "If you have a problem with that, I'll be glad to include your name in the report that I file at the police station after I leave here."

The policeman moved his car and waved them through without another word.

"Way to go, Anita," Joe said, clearly impressed with her performance. "I didn't know that producing TV commercials was such a hard-nosed business."

Anita smiled. "Usually it pays to be nice. The trick is to know when not to be."

As they loaded the Jeep onto the flatbed, Frank picked something up from the ground next to the trailer. "Do you recognize this matchbook?" he asked, handing it to Anita. "It's from a place called Rock Bottom."

"I know that place," Anita said. "It's a club in Vilano Beach. It's kind of seedy. My grandfather would never go there." She thought for a moment. "I'll bet Burt Sculley dropped this."

"You mentioned him yesterday," Frank said. "Who is he again?"

"He's worked for about six months now as first mate on my grandfather's boat. I've never met him, but I spoke to him on the phone once. He said if I ever came to town, he'd take me to Rock Bottom.

"Other than that, all I know is that he's from Australia. I don't know where he lives, and he's not in the phone book. I looked."

"Maybe we should try the club," Joe suggested.

"Good idea," Frank said.

It took two hours to get the Jeep repaired. After paying the mechanic, Anita glanced at her watch. "It's ten-thirty now," she said. "We need to go to the police station, but first I want to drive to my house in Jacksonville. It's over an hour from here, and I want to be there when the mailman arrives."

"Is this because of that great new inflatable lawn chair you ordered, or do you always take your mail this seriously?" Joe asked.

"On the phone my grandfather said he had sent me an important package," Anita explained, ignoring Joe's joke. "But by yesterday, the package hadn't arrived. It could arrive today. If it does, I want to be there."

"I'll bet he sent that package right after he called us," Frank said excitedly. "He hung up just before five because he said he wanted to get to the post office before it closed."

"We'll go with you to Jacksonville," Joe offered. "You said your house was being watched. You might need some protection."

"Thanks, you guys," Anita said. "While we're in Jacksonville, we can also visit Waldo Payne, Grandpa's original partner," Anita added as she drove the Jeep toward Interstate 95. "He'd know where Grandpa is if anybody would."

Just over an hour later, Anita pulled the Jeep up in front of her rented house in Jacksonville. The house was in a neighborhood of small homes built close together among thick, low trees.

"Baloo," Anita cried as her Labrador retriever jumped up to lick her face. "I missed you, too."

The mail hadn't arrived, so Anita sat down on the porch to wait. Sensing that she wanted to be alone, Frank and Joe stayed inside the house.

Fifteen minutes later, Frank and Joe were out back playing with Baloo when they heard Anita calling. They ran to the porch, where the young woman stood clutching a package.

"It's from my grandfather!" Anita tore open the wrapping and pulled out a tattered brown leather book. "This is his journal," she explained, holding the heavy volume as if it was a priceless antique. "He has never let anyone read it."

Carefully setting the book down, she looked in the package again and pulled out a folded sheet of paper. Anita read the note in silence, then handed it to Joe.

My dear Anita:
　　You must know that you mean everything to me.

Joe stopped reading—this didn't seem to be any of his business—but Anita gestured for him to continue. "Look at the last paragraph," she told him.

The journal explains everything. Even though it was a long time ago, you should remember the location as I describe it.

Joe passed the note to Frank, who read it quickly and handed it back to Anita. "What location is he talking about?" Frank asked.

Anita folded the note carefully and slipped it into her pocket. "I guess we'll have to read the journal to find out."

Suddenly a loud crashing noise came from inside the house. Running inside, Frank saw that somebody had thrown a rock through the window. Glass covered the floor.

"I'll check Baloo out back," Frank called to Joe. "You make sure everything's okay in the front."

Frank ran through the kitchen and went out the side door. The dog was clawing at the back gate, trying to dig through. "Whoa, boy, easy," Frank said, before opening the gate. The dog kept whining.

Then Frank heard Anita scream.

He whirled and charged to the front of the house. He rounded the corner to see a heavy-set man dragging Anita, who was struggling and kicking, toward the open door of a small blue car.

"Anita!" Frank yelled, and began to run toward her. Out of the corner of his eye he saw

Joe lying on the porch. His brother wasn't moving.

Frank had only an instant to make a choice. Hoping Joe would forgive him, he ran across the yard, swung his fist, and landed a solid blow on Anita's attacker, hitting him in the back of the neck. The heavyset man pushed Anita to the ground and whirled to face him, apparently unfazed by Frank's blow.

Then Frank felt something hard hit him in the back of the ribs. Pain ripped through his body as the force knocked him off balance. He caught a movement in the corner of his eye as he fell, and rolled to the side as he landed.

An instant later he saw a baseball bat slam into the spot where he had been a moment before. Frank looked up to see a well-built, mustached man leering at him, still brandishing the bat.

Meanwhile, the heavyset man had grabbed Anita again. "Let me go!" Frank heard her scream as the man pushed her into the car with a final, violent shove.

The man called to his partner. "Carlos, come on! We got her!"

"Just one more swing," Carlos said icily, still standing over Frank. He raised the baseball bat again, ready to bring it down on Frank's head.

Chapter

5

No! FRANK'S MIND SCREAMED in protest as Carlos swung the bat at him. Frank scrambled to dodge the blow, then sprang forward and grabbed the bat in his hand as he drove his shoulder into the big man's gut.

Carlos grunted in surprise, then brought his knee up into Frank's chest. Frank staggered backward, gasping, but doggedly held his grip on the bat, pulling it out of Carlos's hand.

The heavyset man called to his partner again from the backseat of the car. "Carlos! I got her! Now let's go!"

Back on the porch, Joe opened his eyes. For a moment he didn't know where he was. Then he remembered. He was at Anita's house. Out in the yard, he thought he saw his brother, Frank, facing a tall man. He also saw a car.

Then a dog ran barking and snapping across the yard. The tall man ran for the car. Frank and the dog ran after the car as it started to move. Somebody was moving in the backseat of the car.

Joe's vision finally cleared as he snapped awake. Anita was in the backseat of the car! They were kidnapping her! Now clearheaded, he jumped up and ran after the car. Anita must have been putting up a good fight, because the car veered back and forth in the road and slammed into a fire hydrant.

The car started forward again, but not before Frank had jumped and landed, spread-eagled, on the hood. He dug his fingers into the gap between the roof of the car and the front window, struggling to hold on as the car gained speed.

Frank could see Carlos through the windshield, bobbing his head back and forth to see out past him. Anita struggled with the other man in the backseat.

Joe caught up to the car and grabbed the handle of the rear door, pulling as hard as he could. It wouldn't budge. Inside the car, a man grinned out at him.

Suddenly the man's grin disappeared as his forehead slammed against the window, and he slumped back into the seat. Anita must have shoved the man from behind, knocking him unconscious! A second later the door flew open on the other side of the car and Anita tumbled out.

Seeing her, Frank jumped off the hood and landed on the pavement, rolling to a stop against the curb. The car screeched off down the street. Baloo followed, barking, until the car disappeared around the corner.

"Frank! Anita!" Joe called as he ran up. "Are you all right?"

Frank stood up, rubbing his shoulder. "I'm okay."

Anita sat in the street, staring blankly at the pavement. She had a bruise on her forehead and several more on her arms, but she looked otherwise unhurt to Joe.

"I'm okay," Anita insisted. Her breath came in short, quick gasps. "If it weren't for you two, I never would have escaped."

Baloo ran up and jumped into Anita's lap. "Yes, you helped, too," she said, hugging the dog. "You're such a good, brave dog."

Several of the neighbors had now gathered on the street. "I called the police," one woman said as Frank, Joe, and Anita walked slowly back to the house.

"Those guys got my grandfather's journal," Anita moaned as they stepped inside. "Now we'll never find him." Then her face brightened slightly. "They didn't get the note, though."

She pulled the folded note out of her pocket. " 'The journal explains everything,' " she read aloud slowly. " 'Even though it was a long time ago, you should remember the location as I describe it.' "

Anita pressed her face into her hands. "I wish I knew what location he's talking about."

Joe put his hand on Anita's shoulder. "Don't worry. One way or another, we'll find him."

The police came a few minutes later. Anita told them the full story of her grandfather's disappearance, beginning with his phone call two nights before. The attending officer, Darcie Williams, listened to her story.

"Assuming somebody has done something to your grandfather as you say," Williams asked, "why would they try to grab you?"

"They must have wanted the package," Joe answered. "If they jumped Mr. Mann as he was talking to Anita on the phone, they could have overheard him telling her about it. Also, she'd be a witness to the crime, in a way."

Officer Williams gestured toward the police car. "You'd better come down to the station."

Frank, Joe, and Anita spent several hours at the police station. Officer Williams questioned each of them, then made several phone calls.

"The St. Augustine police are searching for

your grandfather in connection with a robbery," she told Anita. "Whether he's a victim or a thief, he's obviously mixed up in something dangerous. I suggest you let the police handle the matter."

Frank, Joe, and Anita thanked Officer Williams and left the police station. "She doesn't know us too well if she thinks we'll let the police handle the matter," Joe said as they drove back to Anita's house.

"I'm with you," Frank said. "Do we still have time to visit Payne?"

Anita nodded. "I hope he still lives in the same place. I haven't seen him for a few years."

They quickly cleaned up the mess in the living room and arranged to leave Baloo with one of the neighbors. Then they climbed into the Jeep, drove several miles across town, and parked in front of a small two-story house.

Nobody answered the bell on the first ring. After they rang again, a woman poked her head out of a downstairs window. When asked about Payne, she pointed to the back. "He's probably taking his daily swim."

They walked around back to the pool, which was surrounded by a high wooden fence. Frank opened the gate and waved Anita in. "Ladies first," he said.

"Oh my gosh," Anita gasped as she went inside. Entering behind her, Frank and Joe followed her gaze.

A body was floating facedown in the still water. Its arms and legs were dangling limply toward the bottom. Despite the bright sunlight, there was a deathly calm in the air. Joe had a sinking feeling in his stomach as he viewed the scene.

Anita gripped Frank's arm. "Do you think he's . . ." She didn't finish the sentence.

Joe dove into the pool, clothes still on. Remembering his lifesaving training, he kept his head above the water and his eyes on the victim. He covered the distance to the floating body in a single stroke, and reached out with both arms, gently but firmly supporting the victim's torso and head to roll him onto his back.

He was taken off guard when an elbow caught him hard on the chin. "Get yer hands off me!" The old man kicked and splashed at Joe with the strength of a much younger man.

"I'm sorry, I thought you were . . . I mean—" Joe took in several mouthfuls of water as he attempted to explain himself. Meanwhile, the man swam to the shallow end of the pool, climbed out, and pointed toward the gate.

"Get outta my pool!" he hollered.

Anita ran up to the man. "We're sorry, but we thought you needed help," she explained. "I'm Alvin Mann's granddaughter."

The man walked toward his towel. "Let me get my hearing aid," he said. He inserted a small device into his ear, then turned to look at her.

"I'm Anita Mann, Alvin Mann's granddaughter," she repeated. "You must be Waldo Payne."

Payne stepped back to size her up. "Well, I'll be— I thought I recognized you. How long has it been?"

Joe had also climbed out of the pool. He apologized again as he and Frank were introduced. "You didn't answer when I yelled."

Payne grunted. "Can't an old man go for a swim in his own backyard without getting mugged? I was doing my breath-holding exercises. You almost gave me a heart attack—and my heart's weak enough already."

Joe looked sheepish as he stood, dripping wet, next to his brother. "I guess my advanced life-saving training just kicked in by instinct."

"What about the training that says you should try throwing a life preserver before jumping into the water with all your clothes on?" Frank said, ribbing him.

"Never mind, no harm was done," Payne told them, pulling on his shirt. "What can I do for you three?"

"My grandfather is missing," Anita said earnestly. "I'm afraid he's in real trouble this time. I think he found U-317."

Payne looked at her. "We've thought that before, and we've always come up empty."

"I think it's for real this time. Grandpa even went to Ted Branson for help in salvaging the wreck. Now Ted is telling the police that Grandpa stole thousands of dollars' worth of equipment."

Payne snorted. "Mann stealing from Branson—that's a good one."

"We think Branson might be framing him," Joe said, "so he can keep the gold for himself."

"Has Grandpa called you recently?" Anita asked Payne.

"I haven't spoken with him for months," Payne answered. "I'm sorry I can't give you any more help."

"Think back to the last time you talked to him," Frank pressed. "Did he say anything about the wreck, or give any clue that might help us find him?"

Suddenly Payne seemed anxious to end the conversation. "If there's nothing else, I really should be going inside," he said. "The missus will be wondering why my swim is taking so long."

"Please call if you think of anything else," Anita said before they left, handing him a piece of paper with her phone number written on it.

"Don't you worry about your grandfather," Payne said. "He's a tough old geezer, just like me." He squeezed her hand. "He's always been very proud of you. Oh, and congratulations on that advertising award. He told me about it."

Payne quickly shook hands with the Hardys, then went inside. Frank, Joe, and Anita walked back to the Jeep. Since Anita seemed tired, Frank offered to drive back to St. Augustine while she rested in the backseat.

"Did it seem to you two that Payne reacted strangely when we questioned him?" Frank asked, once they were back on the highway.

"Payne doesn't have anything to hide," Anita said. "He's Grandpa's oldest friend." Her voice trailed off, and Frank thought she must have drifted off to sleep.

They had almost reached St. Augustine when Anita sat bolt upright. "I know what's bothering me!" she exclaimed. "The award that Payne congratulated me on—I won that last month. But Payne said he hadn't talked to my grandfather for months. How would he know about the award then?"

"Either he exaggerated how long it's been," Frank said, "or else he's lying."

Anita had a message waiting at the motel desk when they returned. Her face clouded with fear as she read the pink slip of paper. "It's from the Coast Guard. I'm supposed to call them right away."

Frank and Joe waited anxiously as Anita went

to her room to place the call. If Mann had been rescued, Frank thought grimly, the message would have been from him.

Anita's voice was shaking when she reappeared. "They've found the wreck of my grandfather's boat several miles offshore," she said. "They haven't found any survivors."

Chapter

6

MANN'S BOAT WAS SUNK! Joe was at a loss for words as he saw tears in Anita's eyes. He wished he could wipe the distress off her face, but for a moment he didn't know what to say.

"I really believed he'd sail up to the dock again," Anita whispered, "and everything would be okay."

"Your grandfather may still be all right," Frank said. "Everybody agrees he's a tough guy."

"Frank's right," Joe said. "We don't know whether he was on the boat when it went down. He may still be alive and need our help."

Anita took a deep breath. "You guys are right," she said. "There's too much at stake to give up now."

"Do they know how it happened?" Frank asked.

"The engine caught fire," Anita answered. "They think it happened several days ago, the night he disappeared."

"We could dive the wreck ourselves," Joe suggested.

"Good idea," Anita said, suddenly filled with determination again. "That's the only way we'll find out what happened."

Her voice was barely a whisper when she went on. "Then we'll find out whether Grandpa was on that boat when it went down.

"I know somebody who can help us," she added. "An old friend of mine runs a dive shop here in town. We used to spend our summers together when we were growing up. It's been a while, but she should remember me."

It was almost 6:00 P.M., but they climbed back into the Jeep, hoping to get to the dive shop before it closed. The shop, Groves's Aquatic, was located on Ponce de Leon Boulevard, not far from Branson's marina.

A young woman was locking up the cash register as they entered. "Sorry, but I'm just about to close," she called without looking up.

Anita planted her hands on her hips. "Now, Gwendolyn Cates. Is that any way to greet an old friend?"

The young woman looked up from the register. "Neester, is that you?"

Gwendolyn was of medium height, very fit, with a suntanned complexion. Frank was struck by her long, dark hair and by her accent, which sounded down-home Virginia, with a trace of attitude.

"You bet it's me," Anita answered. "Frank and Joe Hardy, meet Gwendolyn Cates. Still calling the shots here at the dive shop, huh, Gwen?"

"Tell me about it." Gwen rolled her eyes. "It seems like I've been here my whole life. Mr. Groves still owns the place, but he lets me run it the way I want to nowadays."

Gwen looked closely at Anita. "Are you okay? You don't look good."

"I have to ask you for a favor," Anita answered. She quickly told Gwen about the situation with her grandfather, and about their plan to dive the wreckage of his boat.

"You poor thing, you must be worried sick," Gwen said. "Of course I'll help. But diving the wreck could be difficult this time of year. The weather hasn't been good."

"We have had a lot of rain," Anita admitted.

"I'm not talking about rain," Gwen said. "You know as well as I do that it's the end of hurricane season. Lucky for us they're not predicting any storms in the next few days. I guess we could try for tomorrow morning."

Frank, Joe, and Anita agreed to return early the next morning, then drove back to the motel. It had been a long day, so they had a quick dinner at the cafe, then went back to their rooms.

"Do you think Mann could be alive?" Joe asked as he stretched out in his bed.

"If he was on the boat when it went down, it's a long shot," Frank answered. "But don't give up. Hopefully we'll find out tomorrow what happened."

The next morning they woke at 5:00 A.M. and drove straight to the dive shop without stopping for breakfast. It was a clear day, with just a few clouds, and no rain. Gwen was already filling tanks with compressed air when they arrived.

Joe rubbed his eyes. "Why do divers always start so early in the morning?" he complained. "The ocean is there all day long."

"Quit whining and take those four tanks down to the boat," Gwen told him, smiling at Anita.

"Okay, okay," Joe muttered. Frank chuckled and followed with the other two tanks. A minute later they returned.

"Ready for the next load," Frank said.

Gwen looked puzzled. "There is no next load. Just the four tanks."

"But that's only one dive for each of us," Joe objected.

"No, that's two dives for me, and two dives for Anita," Gwen answered. "You guys aren't diving. This is no time for beginners. We're diving a new and unexplored wreck."

"We're not beginners," Frank said. "We've put in a lot of time underwater, including wreck-diving experience. We can take care of ourselves. Besides, you need us. Four divers can search a wreck site more thoroughly than two."

"It's nothing personal," Gwen said, "but I don't take divers to a new site until I'm familiar with their skills."

"I'll vouch for them," Anita said. "I've seen them in action in the past few days. I think they could handle anything."

After a few minutes Gwen gave in, and Frank and Joe prepared to dive. They both knew that the right equipment could mean the difference between life and death, and they sensed Gwen's eyes on them as they selected masks, fins, and other gear. She seemed satisfied with the practiced manner in which they fitted themselves with tanks and buoyancy control jackets, attached regulators, and tested the air pressure in each tank.

Frank picked up a small gadget that looked like a high-tech wristwatch. "This is great. It's like a dive computer. It automatically tracks dive time, depth, and tank pressure."

Their equipment ready, they all boarded Gwen's thirty-five-foot boat, the *Hokie*. Gwen had gotten the coordinates of the wreck from the Coast Guard, and steered to the site using a LORAN receiver.

"The LORAN system uses pulsed radio signals to track your location," Gwen explained. "It's not that precise, but it will get us to the right area. The Coast Guard should have left a buoy to mark the exact site."

A short while later they sighted the buoy, as expected. Gwen steered the boat to a point nearby and dropped anchor.

On the way, Gwen had reminded Frank and Joe about the dangers of wreck-diving, which could include sharp objects, entanglement in ropes or nets, and dangerous marine creatures. "Diving any wreck is dangerous," she said, "but diving a new wreck can be even more so, because the wreck is likely to be unstable.

"Remember that we stay within the limits of recreational diving. That means no staying down long enough to require decompression stops. I assume you know what that means."

"When you dive, the pressure increases the amount of nitrogen in your blood," Frank answered. "If you surface too fast, the nitrogen expands, forming bubbles in your bloodstream."

"That's right." Gwen nodded, satisfied. "Also, no swimming inside the shipwreck. When you enter the wreck, the stakes go up dramatically."

After dropping anchor, they reviewed their dive plan carefully before gearing up. Frank and Gwen would make the first dive. They would descend along the buoy line and circle the site to get their bearings, and then use their remaining bottom time to explore as much of the wreck as they could. Joe and Anita would remain onboard until Frank and Gwen had returned to the boat, and then make their dive.

Joe and Anita helped Frank and Gwen to pull on their wet suits, weight belts, fins, and other gear, then finally their BC jackets and air tanks. After double-checking their pressure gauges and regulators, Frank and Gwen were ready to go.

Frank felt like a seal as he waddled backward to the ladder and lowered himself over the rear of the boat. He knew that a smooth entry could be important, not only to avoid losing one's equipment, but to avoid disturbing the wreck site below.

Once in the water, a strong current pulled him toward the marker buoy. He grabbed the buoy rope without difficulty and waited for Gwen. Then, with a thumbs-down signal to let Gwen know he was descending, he sank beneath the surface.

Light beamed down, coloring the water a rich

greenish blue that darkened as they descended. Frank could still feel the current pulling at him, but after the roughness of the surface, the sudden quiet was a relief. The mechanical sound of his own breathing filled his ears.

As Frank reached the bottom, he added a quick blast of air to his buoyancy control jacket to stop his descent. His depth gauge read fifty-one feet. Neutral buoyancy was a wonderful thing, he thought to himself. By adding the right amount of air to his BC jacket, he could hover effortlessly above the bottom without kicking up any sand. If he breathed in, he'd float up just slightly. Breathing out caused him to sink back down.

Frank looked around as Gwen descended next to him. He could already see the sunken boat leaning to one side on the sandy bottom. The boat itself looked forlorn, and worse, he was afraid of what they might find inside. Had Alvin Mann gone down with his ship?

They circled the wreck as they had planned, starting with the stern and moving in a clockwise direction. As they approached the bow they could see the damage caused by the fire. A large section of the hull had burned away on the starboard, or right, side, just behind the bow.

Frank tried to piece together the boat's last moments in his mind as he grimly examined the burned hull. The fire had started near the engine, and must have been fast and sudden. But what had happened to Mann? Had anyone else been onboard? There were no answers yet, and a glance at his dive computer showed that they were running low on air.

Back on deck they described what they had seen to Joe and Anita, who had waited tensely the whole time Frank and Gwen were underwater.

"It looks like the fire started suddenly and spread fast," Frank told them. "My guess is that it was an explosion, but there's no way to tell what caused it."

A few minutes later Joe and Anita were ready to go. "You two be careful down there," Gwen called out as they lowered themselves into the water. "And remember, don't swim inside the wreck."

Joe held his nose and blew out through his ears as he descended, in order to equalize the pressure. As with Frank, the sudden quiet and the sensation of weightlessness thrilled him almost as much as the opportunity for underwater discovery—even though both he and Anita were fearful of what they might find on this particular dive.

Reaching the bottom, they swam over the top of the boat and searched the deck and upper cabin. The front of the cabin had burned away, and all but one of the cabin windows had been shattered. Looks like an explosion, all right, Joe thought grimly.

A portion of the upper deck had burned away, exposing the engine compartment. Joe swam toward it. This didn't count as going *inside* the wreck, he figured. Anita followed.

The burned remains of the boat's hull arced up on both sides. The engine itself was mangled by fire. Joe spotted something lodged in the wooden side. It looked like a portion of a steel gas tank. The gas tank must have exploded, he thought.

Joe turned to show Anita what he had found, but she had already swum farther into the cabin. He followed, swimming carefully between the shards of broken glass and metal.

He was pretty sure what they were doing wasn't a good idea. The burned remains of the cabin looked as if they could cave in at any moment.

Joe swam to Anita, who was peering into an open doorway that led to a stairway going down into the boat.

Joe knew what Anita was thinking. Despite Gwen's warning, she was going to search the entire boat. If her grandfather's remains—or any other clues to his whereabouts—were onboard, she was going to find them. Joe couldn't help but admire her determination.

Joe shone his light down the stairway, his heart thumping. Despite his better judgment, he was thinking about swimming down into the inner cabin.

Then his beam froze on something that made his heart jump. Anita saw it, too. She gripped his shoulder tightly.

They were looking at a human hand.

Joe forced himself to remain calm. Beside him, Anita was panicking. He mouthed the words "Calm down!" pulling his regulator out of his mouth, but she was out of control now. She thrashed with her arms and legs, kicking up silt and knocking her tank against the wall as she tried to swim deeper into the cabin.

Then things went from bad to worse. Joe watched in horror as a section of burned wall and glass collapsed, trapping Anita. She struggled to free herself, dangerously close to jagged pieces of glass that could cut her or damage her equipment.

Joe swam to Anita and grabbed her by the shoulders. He could see the fear in her eyes. "Relax!" he mouthed, removing the regulator again quickly, even though his own heart was pounding.

His grip seemed to calm her. She closed her eyes and gradually slowed her breathing. Joe tried to relax, too, but only for a moment.

The water around them darkened with blood.

In her thrashing, Anita had cut her arm on the broken glass. The cut could be serious, and even if it wasn't, it could attract sharks, Joe knew.

His heart still thumping, Joe set to work to free Anita without doing further damage. Another cut on the glass—or a cut on her air hose—could be disastrous.

Then a shadow passed over them. Anita saw it, too. Once again her eyes filled with fear. Looking up, Joe followed her gaze. A large shark was circling over them.

Joe steeled himself as the shark swam directly at them, mouth gaping.

Chapter

7

JOE STARED AT THE ROWS of glistening teeth in the shark's huge mouth as it came at him. It was only a few arm's lengths away, and moving fast.

Only a few more feet.

Joe forced himself to freeze. Sharks had poor eyesight, he knew, but were attracted to movement. Even the bubbles from his regulator might attract the fish's attention. Humans weren't supposed to be very tasty to sharks—but this particular shark might not know that yet.

Joe ducked at the last instant. The shark swept past him, inches from his face, then clamped its jaws on a partly burned timber that had once been part of the cabin wall. The whole boat shook as the shark thrashed its head back and forth until the wood broke. The shark swam away, part of the broken board still in its mouth.

Joe looked down at Anita. She was still trapped under the wreckage, but she had had the presence of mind to pull her wet suit over the cut, so that the shark might not smell the blood so quickly. With her free hand, she was applying pressure to control the bleeding.

Joe struggled to free her from the glass and debris as the shark circled and came at them again. Joe grabbed a section of broken timber.

He held the board in front of him with both hands and braced his feet against the deck, remembering what his football coach had told him—if you're going to take a hit, tuck your head and deliver one instead.

The shark closed again. At the last second, Joe drove forward with his legs, ramming the timber into the shark's mouth and pushing the shark's head away from him at the same time.

The shark changed course, veering off with the board in its mouth. Joe and Anita watched tensely as it circled several more times, then finally disappeared into the murky distance.

With the shark gone, Joe finally managed to free Anita. He pointed upward with his thumb, giving the signal to surface.

Anita shook her head and pointed to the doorway that led to the lower cabin. Joe had to admire her courage. Despite the danger, she had to know what—or who—was down at the bottom of the stairway.

They swam back to the doorway and looked down the stairs again. The hand was still there, floating in the darkness. Moving feet first, Joe maneuvered down for a closer look, shining his light ahead of him.

Relief surged through his body when he realized what the floating object was, and he held it up for Anita to see. It was a glove.

They could finally surface, but they still forced themselves to go slowly, keeping their eyes out for the shark. Joe gulped in the air greedily the instant his head broke the surface, thinking that fresh air had never tasted so good. Anita's head popped up a second later.

Joe expected to feel a bite on his legs at any moment as they swam back to the boat. Only when both of them were safely on deck again did he let out a sigh of relief.

Frank and Gwen listened with concern as Joe and Anita told their story. Though relieved the pair were safe, Gwen was upset at what had happened. "Nobody was supposed to go inside the wreck," she said. "As dive master, I'm responsible. If we're going to dive again, I need to know that all of us will stick to the plan."

"It was my fault," Anita said as Gwen bandaged the cut on her arm. "Nothing would have happened if I hadn't panicked. Anyway, we found out what we needed to know."

There was no more conversation as they hauled up the anchor and steered the boat toward shore. All four of them were alone with their thoughts. They all knew that Anita's last comment wasn't quite true.

In spite of their efforts, they hadn't found anything conclusive, Joe thought. Maybe Mann had gone down with his boat, and maybe he hadn't. All they knew for sure was that he was still missing and he was still wanted by the police. And, Joe thought grimly, the men who had stolen his journal and tried to kidnap Anita were still on the loose.

The sun was low in the sky by the time they pulled up to the dock and cut the engine. Only then did Frank break the silence.

"There's one player in all this that we still haven't talked to," he said. "Your grandfather's assistant, Burt Sculley. Where is he now? If he sees your grandfather regularly, he has to know something."

"I don't know how to find him," Anita said. "He's not listed in the phone book, and when I called directory assistance they couldn't tell me anything either. He's from Australia, and I don't think he's a legal resident of the U.S. I think Grandpa just paid him cash, under the table, on a per-job basis."

"What about those matches we found near your uncle's trailer?" Joe asked. "They were from some local club where you said we might find him."

"The club is called Rock Bottom," Anita said. "I've only been there once, and I promised myself I'd never go back. It's a pretty raucous place."

"It'll be okay if we're with you," Frank said. "We should go there tonight, if possible. It's not much, but it's a lead."

Anita sighed. "All right. But let's head back to the motel, then. If we're going to do up the town, I need to dress for the occasion."

After helping Gwen unload the tanks and other gear from the boat, the Hardys and Anita got into the Jeep and drove back to their motel. Frank and Joe had a quick dinner in the cafe while Anita disappeared into her room, saying she'd be ready soon.

Over an hour later, they were still waiting for her. "She sure is taking a long time," Joe complained, pacing back and forth.

But when she finally appeared, Joe decided that it was worth the wait. "You look great," he blurted, knowing that Vanessa, the girl he dated back in Bayport, would have elbowed him in the ribs if she'd seen his reaction.

Anita was wearing a short black dress. Her hair was combed back, and her brown eyes were accented with a touch of mascara. "Ready to roll?" She smiled.

They piled into the Jeep and drove south to Vilano Beach. Rock Bottom was well named, Frank couldn't help thinking as they parked in front of the club, a run-down wooden building. Loud music came from inside, along with occasional shouts and, once, the crash of breaking glass.

"Having second thoughts about going in?" Anita asked. But Frank and Joe didn't hesitate. They needed to find Burt Sculley, and this place was their only lead.

Inside, music pounded from the jukebox. For all the noise, there weren't that many people, Joe noticed. The place was still getting warmed up for the night. There were only a few people on the dance floor, while several others sat at tables, laughing and talking loudly. In back, a guy played pool by himself.

Joe and Anita moved toward the dance floor while Frank walked to the pool table. The guy was practicing elaborate trick shots, trying to bounce the balls off walls and corners. None of the shots went in.

After a few minutes the guy turned to Frank. His face was fleshy and round. "Interested in a game?" Frank nodded as he racked the balls.

"I'm Stan," the guy said as he took his first

shot, spreading the balls around the table. None went in. "Not from around here, are you?"

Frank ignored the question as he shot, sinking his first ball. He sank two more balls, then missed a shot and stepped back from the table. "I'm looking for Burt Sculley," he said casually. "Have you seen him tonight?"

Stan gave him a sharp look. "Who wants to know?"

Frank tried to hide his excitement. "I have a friend who's trying to put together a crew," he answered. "I heard Sculley might be looking for work."

"I haven't seen him yet tonight," Stan answered. "But if you stick around, he might show up."

The game went on. Stan kept missing his shots and was starting to get surly as Frank knocked in ball after ball and finally dropped the eight ball to win the game. "We play again," Stan said, "but first I need to make a phone call."

Frank agreed. He wasn't too impressed with Stan's winning personality, but this guy knew Sculley. As long as there was a chance of finding out more, he wanted the game to continue. While Stan made his call, Frank drifted over to the dance floor to let Joe and Anita know what was happening.

Stan came back and the game continued.

Frank tried several times to ask questions about Sculley, but Stan kept avoiding them. All he would say was that Sculley might be in later. Meanwhile Frank won two more games, and Stan was getting increasingly annoyed.

"There's a better table in the back room," Stan said after the third game. "Let's go play there."

"What's wrong with this table?" Frank asked.

Stan slammed his cue down on the table. "I insist," he said. "Besides, there's somebody back there you might want to meet."

That got Frank's interest. He shot a glance across the room to where Joe and Anita were dancing, wanting to tell them where he was going, but Stan was already disappearing down the back hallway. Frank hesitated a moment, then followed.

Stan walked to the end of the hallway and opened a door. "In here," he said.

"Wait a minute," Frank said. He could see that the doorway led to a large utility closet, empty except for a few mops and other supplies. "No offense, but I like the atmosphere better out—"

Before he could finish, somebody grabbed him from behind. One arm went around his neck, and another grabbed his right arm. Frank pushed back with his left elbow and heard a grunt as he made contact.

Stan stepped forward and punched Frank in the stomach. Frank reeled forward, gasping for breath, but Stan grabbed him by the hair and yanked his head back up.

Bleary-eyed, Frank struggled against the arms that still held him from behind as Stan drew his fist back to deliver what would be a knockout punch. But the blow never came.

Instead, Frank felt the cold, sharp blade of a knife pressed against his throat. Knowing that any false move would be his last, he went limp and allowed himself to be dragged into the closet. Stan followed, locking the door behind them and turning on the light.

Frank still couldn't see who was holding the knife against his throat. "Guys, if this is about my winning the pool game, I'm sure we can work something out," he said, trying to stall for time while he figured out what was going on.

"Shut up!" Stan bellowed, whacking Frank in the face with the back of his hand.

The man holding the knife finally spoke up. He had a strong accent that Frank recognized as Australian. "Give me one good reason why I shouldn't cut your throat."

Despite his predicament, Frank had to struggle to hide his excitement. His attacker had to be Burt Sculley!

Chapter

8

FRANK HAD TO THINK FAST. Sculley wanted to cut his throat, and he didn't even know why.

He knew that he had been stupid to follow Stan without telling Joe where he was going. With the music pounding through the club, calling for help now would be useless.

Sculley pressed the knife even closer against his throat. "Give me one reason why I shouldn't kill you," he repeated, louder than before.

Frank decided that acting as if he didn't know what was going on would make Sculley even angrier.

"Look, Sculley, I know you're mad," he said, "but we can talk this out."

"You and your friends should have thought

of that before you trashed my place and threatened to kill me," Sculley snapped.

"What—" Frank began, but Sculley yanked his arm, spinning him around. Stan grabbed his other arm and the two men pinned him against the wall as Sculley pointed the knife at Frank's chest. He was smaller than Frank, with short hair and a long, straight nose.

"You pushed me too far," Scully growled. "Now I'm fighting back."

Outside, something slammed hard against the door of the closet. The lock held, but the noise made Sculley and Stan whirl around.

The distraction gave Frank the moment he needed. He heaved up with both arms, grabbing Sculley's knife arm with one hand and catching Stan's jaw with the other. Stan fell backward as Sculley pushed against Frank's grip, using both hands to try and drive the knife down into Frank's chest.

Then the door crashed open. Joe flew into the room and plowed into Sculley, knocking him forward. Frank barely managed to deflect the knife so that it went harmlessly past him as Sculley tumbled to the ground, Joe on top of him.

Spinning around, Frank landed a kick in Stan's gut. Stan staggered backward, scrambled for his balance, and ran out the door.

Joe hauled Sculley to his feet and slammed him up against the wall, pinning him.

"You okay?" Joe asked.

"I am now," Frank answered.

Anita stuck her head in the door. "Are you boys having fun in there?"

Joe gave her a wink. "We just need a few minutes of quality time in here. Close the door behind you, and give us a warning knock if anyone comes."

Instead Anita joined them in the closet, shutting the door behind her. Frank and Joe were startled by the cold expression on her face.

She glared at Sculley as Frank and Joe searched him. "Where is my grandfather?"

"Your grandfather?" Understanding came slowly into Sculley's eyes. "You must be Anita. I thought you were—" His voice trailed off.

"You thought we were what?" Frank demanded.

Sculley stared at the floor until Joe grabbed his shirt, towering over him, eyes blazing. "I've just about lost my temper," Joe growled. "I'm tired of being run over, threatened, and generally pushed around. A man's life is at stake."

Sculley looked scared. "I really don't know where your grandfather is," he said to Anita. "I haven't seen him since we found—" His voice trailed off again.

Joe tightened his grip on Sculley's shirt. "Found what?"

"I'm not even sure. Some submarine wreck. Then everything went out of control."

Joe released his grip. "Start from the beginning."

Sculley sighed. "I've been working with Mann for about six months. Mostly we do routine salvage work, but Mann is also on a mission to find some German submarine from World War II.

"Several months ago I met a guy named Demas," Sculley went on. "He knew about the submarine, and offered to pay me for regular reports on our work, with a nice bonus if we ever found the submarine. I figured it was easy money, and we'd never find the sub, anyhow."

"You took money to spy," Joe said with disgust.

Sculley shifted uneasily. "Last Sunday we found the submarine—by sheer luck, miles south of where we'd been looking. Mann said it was funny, because it was a place he'd dived lots of times before, near some place he called Skeleton Rock."

"Skeleton *Key* Rock," Anita corrected him excitedly. "I know that rock. About twenty-two miles offshore, southeast of town, right?"

Sculley nodded, surprised.

"I'm the one who named it Skeleton Key," she added. "That's what it looked like. There's a little cave you can swim into, and—never mind." She looked embarrassed as she saw that everyone was staring at her.

Sculley continued his story. "After we found the submarine, I called Demas. He wanted me to tell him the location right over the phone, but I refused. I wanted my money first, so I arranged another meeting."

"What happened?" Joe asked.

"I never went. Some hunch told me it might not be a good idea. Demas always made me nervous, and when I told him we'd found the submarine, his tone changed. I heard greed in his voice. After that, they ransacked my apartment. I've been in hiding ever since."

Sculley turned to Anita as he finished. "The next day, your grandfather disappeared. I'm afraid Demas and his gang got to him. I really am sorry. I never thought anybody would get hurt."

"You betrayed him all the same," Joe growled.

"How did you get in touch with Demas?" Frank asked Sculley.

"He gave me a phone number to call," Sculley answered. "Sometimes he'd pick up, but usually I just left a message on an answering machine."

"Can you call Demas and arrange a meeting for tomorrow morning?" Frank asked.

Sculley shook his head. "I'm not going near those guys again."

"We insist," Joe said. "We'll go with you. Schedule the meeting in a public place, and you should be fine."

"You better be careful who you get mixed up with," Sculley said. "These people are trouble. Demas isn't the worst. He's just a small fish."

"What do you mean?" Joe asked.

"The first time I met Demas was in a parking lot. There was somebody else there who stayed in the car—somebody who seemed important. Even Demas was scared of him. Every minute or two Demas would walk over to the car and speak to him through the window, which was rolled down just a crack."

"You know, you can't hide forever," Frank told Sculley. "We can help you get these guys off your back."

Without waiting for an answer, they dragged Sculley to a pay phone and refused to budge until he made the call. They didn't see any sign of Stan—apparently he had run out for good.

"Okay, you've got your meeting," Sculley told them as he hung up the phone. "Tomorrow morning at 10 at Alligator World."

"Alligator World?" Joe repeated.

"It's a theme park in St. Augustine, like a minizoo," Anita explained.

"Demas insisted that we meet there," Sculley said. "In front of Cayman's cage."

"Who's Cayman?" Frank asked.

Anita smiled. "You'll find out tomorrow."

As they left Rock Bottom, Sculley started to walk away, saying he'd see them the following morning. Frank pulled him back by the arm.

"Why don't you spend the night with us, in our motel?" he suggested.

"Thanks, but—"

"Really, we insist," Joe added, giving Sculley a slight shove and a broad smile. He knew it would be a long night because he and Frank would have to take turns watching Sculley. They couldn't risk letting him out of their sight, though.

"Fair enough," Sculley said. "I like a comfortable room with a nice bed, and in the morning I like a hot shower, followed by breakfast from room service."

"I'll give you a hot shower," Joe muttered. "You'll be *sleeping* in the shower if you're not careful."

As Joe feared, it was a long night. The next morning Sculley was the only one who seemed well-rested. "Best sleep I've had in days," he said, beaming. "With you two keeping watch, I slept like a baby."

Sculley took so much time in the shower that he used up all the hot water, forcing Frank and

Joe to take cold showers. Frank was afraid that they would be late for their 10:00 A.M. meeting, but they arrived at Alligator World with several minutes to spare.

Frank and Joe talked Anita out of going with them to meet Demas. "Demas won't know who Joe and I are, and that will keep him guessing," Frank had told her. "If you went, he'd probably recognize you or guess who you were."

"Drop us off a block or two away, and wait in the Jeep," Joe suggested. "Be ready to make a quick pickup when we come out. We may be in a hurry."

Frank and Joe stayed close to Sculley as they walked to the ticket booth, where a large sign announced the main attraction: Meet Cayman, Florida's Largest Captive Alligator.

"Two, please," Frank said to the attendant.

"You're not paying for my ticket?" Sculley objected.

Frank sighed. "Make that three."

"At least we know who Cayman is," Joe said as they went through the gate. The compound was enclosed by a fence but open to the outside air. A series of paths and bridges thick with foliage connected swamp exhibits filled with turtles, lizards, and crocodiles.

Frank pointed to an area where a crowd was ming. "That must be Cayman's cage."

"No sign of Demas yet. I guess he's not coming," Sculley said.

Joe looked at his watch. "Don't get your hopes up. It's just ten now."

As they joined the crowd, Joe saw several people looking eagerly at their watches, obviously waiting for something. "What's the big event?" he asked a man standing nearby.

"Cayman's ten A.M. feeding," the man answered. "He's a monster. It's really something to see those jaws in action."

The Hardys and Sculley moved to the far end of the cage, where the crowd was thinner, and stepped up to the rail for a look. The alligator was only half out of the water, its rear legs and tail in the swamp, but they could see that the beast was huge.

"He must be almost twenty-five feet long," Frank said. The alligator rested in the sun, eyes closed. Several teeth protruded out of its mouth, forming an evil-looking grin.

"He looks too lazy to be dangerous," Joe commented.

"Don't fool yourself," Frank answered. "Alligators can move amazingly fast. But they usually don't attack humans."

"That's what you told me about sharks," Joe muttered.

Looking around the crowd, Frank recognized the heavyset man who had tried to kidnap Anita from her house in Jacksonville. "Is that Demas?" he asked Sculley, who nodded.

Joe looked where they were pointing, but all he saw was a uniformed guard clearly cautioning a woman not to allow her little boy to stand on the railing.

"Where's Demas?" Joe asked.

"Behind the guard," Frank said.

Demas moved toward them, a broad grin on his face, and walked right up to Sculley. "Glad you finally decided to call us," he said. Then he noticed Frank and Joe. "Hey, what are you two doing here?"

Before they could answer, Sculley lunged at Demas. "You set me up!" he shouted. Demas jumped aside, and Sculley flew into the crowd, knocking over several people.

"What're you trying to pull?" A large man bristled at Sculley, who jumped up and made a break for it, followed by the man and several others. The security guard followed, blowing his whistle.

Demas turned and ran in the other direction. Frank and Joe followed as Demas shoved his way roughly through the crowd.

"Move it, lady." Demas plowed between the woman and her little boy, who was still standing on the railing, bumping the kid in the process.

The woman screamed as her son tottered on the railing, trying to regain his balance. As

Frank and Joe watched in horror, the boy fell over the rail, right into Cayman's cage!

"Noah!" the woman screamed.

Frank and Joe ran to the rail. The little boy splashed around in the mud, crying. The alligator was awake now, its eyes fixed on little Noah.

"Mommy!" Noah screamed. The alligator slunk out of the water toward the little boy.

Joe looked around frantically. The security guard had gone after Sculley, and everybody else in the crowd seemed hypnotized by what was happening inside the cage. All the while, the alligator was moving closer. Joe had to do something fast, or the child would be killed.

Joe sprang over the rail, landing on his hands and knees in the mud about ten feet away from the frightened child.

"Over here!" he called, trying to draw the big beast's attention. The alligator turned to look at him, opening and closing its jaws, then darted forward, coming between Joe and the little boy. Joe was amazed how fast it had moved. It was barely ten feet from him now.

Then, snapping its jaws, the alligator charged right at him.

Chapter

9

WHEN CAYMAN CHARGED, Joe did the only thing he could think of.

He ran straight toward it.

Not the best plan, he realized, but he didn't have any time to think of a better one. Besides, he thought this might surprise the alligator, which, Joe figured, probably wasn't used to being charged.

With Cayman closing fast from the other direction, it took only one step to close the gap. Then Joe sprang into the air. The jaws snapped at him, missing his legs by inches as he hurtled right over the alligator's head.

He landed on his feet, tumbled in the mud, rolled back onto his feet, and ran for the far side of the compound, scooping up the little boy along the way. Reaching the side of the compound, he stood on his toes and held the child up to the onlookers who stretched their arms toward the little boy's hand. They were inches short.

The alligator turned to face Joe again, its long tail sweeping back and forth through the mud as it rotated its body.

On the other side of the rail, Frank saw the alligator turn to face his brother.

"Hey, Cayman!" he called, trying to draw its attention. He grabbed an empty bottle from a trash bin and threw it as hard as he could. It landed inches from Cayman's jaw but didn't seem to have any effect. The alligator advanced toward Joe. Joe was still holding up the child.

Gritting his teeth, Frank jumped over the rail into the compound. "Hey, lizard breath—over here!" he called, jumping up and down to draw the reptile's attention.

His diversion worked. The alligator turned and charged him. Luckily, Frank hadn't gone far from the wall. He turned and jumped for the rail, barely making it over before the alligator got to him.

Frank's diversion had given Joe the time he needed. He finally stretched high enough to pass the child off, then leaped over the rail himself.

The crowd swarmed around Frank and Joe as

the woman clutched her child in her arms. "Thank you, thank you," she gasped. "How can I ever repay you?"

"I'm just happy he's safe," Joe answered modestly. He realized he was covered with mud from the compound.

Frank looked around for any sign of Sculley or Demas. "Did anybody see where that guy went after he bumped the child?" he asked several people.

A man wearing a blue suit appeared. "I'm Mr. Bellows, the general manager," he announced to the crowd. "Let me assure everyone that Alligator World is committed to the safety of its guests. A thorough investigation will be conducted."

Nobody seemed to listen to him. All eyes were still on the Hardys. "Can I have your autograph?" a teenage girl asked Joe.

Another man stuck a video camera into Joe's face. "How did you feel when the gator came at you?" he asked.

Joe pushed the camera aside and followed Frank out of the park. Several people from the crowd followed them as they ran down the street toward the Jeep.

"Wait!" someone called. "What are your names? You'll be famous!"

Anita started the engine and threw open the door as they ran up. Then she saw Joe's mud-covered shorts. "You're not getting into my Jeep with all that mud," she objected.

Joe ignored her. "Hit the gas," he said, climbing in after Frank.

"What in the world happened?" Anita asked.

"Joe entered an alligator-wrestling contest." Frank grinned. "The alligator won."

Anita rolled her eyes. "Typical. He sees a mud puddle, he jumps in."

"Did you see Sculley or Demas come out?" Joe asked, changing the subject.

"Sculley came out a few minutes ago, but I waited because I didn't see you guys," Anita said. "He ran across the parking lot and behind that restaurant," she said, pointing to the far end of the parking lot.

"Maybe we can still catch him," Frank said. But after driving around for several minutes, they gave up. A crowd had formed outside Alligator World, and they didn't want to be caught in the mob.

"Let's get out of here," Joe said. "I don't want to spend the rest of the day being interviewed by everyone on the planet."

"Where to?" Anita asked.

"How about Gwen's shop?" Frank suggested. "I think we need to plan another dive."

Gwen was behind the counter, wrestling with the computer, when they arrived. "I hate this thing," she complained. Then she noticed the mud covering Joe. "Don't go tramping that mud through my store," she said. "There's a shower in back that we use to rinse off the scuba gear. You can clean up there."

Joe went to rinse off, glad it was a warm, sunny day. By the time he returned, Frank had told Gwen and Anita about the dramatic rescue at the alligator park.

"You'll be famous," Gwen told him. "Everybody around here knows Cayman."

"We ran out without giving our names," Joe said. "We were still hoping to catch up with Sculley and Demas, but we lost both of them."

"At least we have a better idea who we're up against," Frank said. "Sculley's friend Demas is one of the two guys who tried to kidnap Anita and grabbed the journal. Of course, we don't know who Demas works for," he added, remembering what Sculley had said about somebody important who stayed in the car.

"Sculley gave us the location of the submarine, U-317," Joe said. "That's the only real clue we've got. The submarine wreck has to be the key to this whole mystery. If we can find that place Sculley mentioned—Skeleton Key Rock— then maybe we can blow this whole mystery wide open."

Gwen unfolded several nautical charts. "Skeleton Key Rock isn't marked on any of these charts," she said.

"That was just a name that my grandfather and I used," Anita said. "Do you remember that time years ago when we dived with my grandfather and I lost my new diving knife? That was it."

Gwen nodded. "I'll check my old diving logbooks. Back then I used a sextant to record the locations of my dives. If I've been there before, I can find it."

They agreed to dive the next morning, weather permitting. That meant they had the rest of the day free.

"I'd like to find out more about U-317," Frank said. "How it was sunk, stuff like that. I'll bet the local library would have old news clippings on file."

The library was located just north of the historic district, next to a park with a merry-go-round. "We've got every issue of the St. Augustine *Gazette* since July 1922 on microfilm," the librarian told them.

He led them to a large machine that looked like a giant version of the hand-held viewer Frank remembered their father using to examine old slides.

"I haven't used one of these in a while," Frank said.

The librarian was surprised. "Most young people today don't even know what microfilm is. Nowadays everybody expects everything to be published on the World Wide Web."

Frank was already moving through the stacks. Opening a long drawer, he pulled out several boxes containing strips of film that looked like large photographic negatives. He threaded one of the rolls onto spools below the viewer, and the image of a newspaper page was projected on the screen.

Joe glanced at the page. "Nothing about our submarine there."

Frank slipped in another film. "Here it is," he said after a minute. " 'U-boat sunk off St. Augustine.' " The others crowded around as he read aloud:

"A combined force of Coast Guard and Navy planes sunk an unidentified German U-boat yesterday approximately twenty-six miles northeast of St. Augustine.

"The enemy sub disappeared under the waves after being hit by the planes of the 14th squadron. They tried escaping to the north, but the U.S.S. *McHenry* gave chase, pounding the enemy with depth charges until the kill was confirmed by oil and other wreckage. The entire crew went down with their ship."

The article was dated June 13, 1944.

Joe let out a deep breath, struck by the matter-of-fact tone in which so many deaths were reported.

"There was one survivor," Anita said. "I told you about him before. He's the one who started this whole affair, at least as far as my grandfather was concerned. Grandpa's boat picked him up. He was the only prisoner of war here in St. Augustine."

"You're right," Frank said, looking at an article from two days later:

German Survivor Rescued

The U.S.S. *McHenry* last night rescued a German seaman, identified as First Officer Klaus Krueger of the German submarine U-317.

Presumed to be a survivor of the unidentified U-boat sunk two days earlier, Krueger had been severely burned and suffered from delirium after more than twenty-six hours at sea.

Krueger was taken to Menendez Hospital, where his condition is listed as critical.

Authorities hope that, if Krueger survives, he may be able to provide an explanation for the presence of the submarine in U.S. waters, considered highly unusual at this stage of the war.

"Krueger died without giving away any answers," Anita said. "He never made it out of the hospital. From what I heard, he was comatose by the time he got there and lasted only a day or two."

Frank rewound the roll of microfilm. "I wonder if anybody at the hospital still remembers him."

"It's a long shot, but we could go ask," Anita suggested. "The hospital isn't far from here."

Menendez Hospital was a large concrete building built in the Spanish style popular in St. Augustine. Anita parked the Jeep beneath a row of palm trees that lined the front.

The female receptionist smiled at them as they walked in. Anita said that they were doing a history project on Krueger, St. Augustine's only prisoner of war during World War II.

The receptionist scratched her head. "If anybody in the hospital would remember him, it would be Mrs. Pritchett. She's our custodian of hospital records. Room 108, down the hall."

"Will they still have Krueger's records on file after all these years?" Anita asked.

The receptionist smiled again. "Honey, it wouldn't surprise me if they had records going back all the way to the Revolutionary War. Mrs. Pritchett is very efficient."

Following her directions, they walked to room

108 and knocked on the door. A minute later an elderly woman opened the door.

"You must be Mrs. Pritchett," Anita said.

They understood now what the receptionist had meant. The gray-haired Mrs. Pritchett looked as if she'd spent quite a few years at the library. But she smiled warmly as she waved them into the office filled with tall file cabinets, offering them tea.

"Yes, I remember when poor Krueger came to the hospital," Mrs. Pritchett said in answer to their question. "But it's funny that you're asking about him today."

"What do you mean?" Frank asked.

"Just a few weeks ago, Krueger's nephew came and made copies of all his files," she answered. "He said he wanted them for the family archives."

Joe leaned forward. "What did he look like?"

Mrs. Pritchett thought for a moment. "He was tall and very nicely dressed. That's all I remember."

"May we see Krueger's chart?" Frank asked.

"I don't see why not," Mrs. Pritchett answered. "Usually we release records only to family members, but after so many years, I don't suppose it matters."

She walked to one of the file cabinets. "It was terrible what happened to him," she said. "The poor man was burned all over his body, and survived only a few days after he came here.

"He was the only prisoner of war we ever had at the hospital, and nobody knew how to deal with him. The authorities wanted to give him an armed guard, but we refused. Even though there was a war on, we wanted him to die in peace.

"Here it is." She pulled out a chart and set it on the table before them.

Frank and Joe looked over Anita's shoulder as she opened the folder and paged slowly through the documents, wincing at the details of Krueger's final days. "Here's the death certificate," Anita said.

Suddenly she sat bolt upright, her eyes widening. "This can't be!" she exclaimed. She pointed at the bottom of the page. "Take a look at the signature."

Frank and Joe leaned over the table to see where she was pointing. They blinked with surprise as they recognized the name the signature spelled out.

The death certificate was signed by Waldo Payne, Alvin Mann's original partner!

Chapter 10

"THIS MUST BE A MISTAKE!" Anita exclaimed. "How could Waldo Payne have signed the death certificate? He was a sailor, not a doctor."

Mrs. Pritchett went to a different file cabinet and pulled out another folder. "Actually, he was neither," she said. "According to our employee records, he was an orderly. He worked here from 1944 through 1946."

"It doesn't make sense," Anita insisted. "Waldo Payne was in the Coast Guard, just like my grandfather. They became friends right after the war."

"Perhaps you're thinking of a different Waldo Payne," Mrs. Pritchett suggested.

"That would be a pretty amazing coincidence," Joe said. "Is it possible that he could have been in the Coast Guard *and* worked at the hospital?"

Frank was puzzled about something else. "Isn't a death certificate supposed to be signed by a doctor rather than an orderly? Who was the attending physician?"

Frank flipped through the chart, reading off the names of several doctors. "Are any of them still here?"

Mrs. Pritchett shook her head. "They all retired years ago. I don't know where any of them are now."

They studied the records for several more minutes, but didn't find anything else unusual. Thanking Mrs. Pritchett, they left the hospital.

"Payne has some explaining to do," Anita said as they climbed back into the Jeep. "He sure never told my grandfather that he signed Krueger's death certificate." She shuddered. "That seems like kind of a major detail to omit."

"Where are we going?" Joe asked as Anita pulled the Jeep out of the parking lot and pointed it away from St. Augustine.

"To Jacksonville," Anita answered. "To have another talk with Waldo Payne."

Despite the rush-hour traffic, they reached Payne's apartment before the sun had set. Once again Payne didn't answer his door, and this time he wasn't in the pool out back either. They decided to have dinner and try again.

Several hours later Payne still wasn't answering his door. In the meantime, they had gone to Anita's house to pick up the mail and had stopped at her neighbor's house to visit Baloo. It was getting late.

Frank looked at his watch. "We should get back to St. Augustine. Remember, we're supposed to dive tomorrow morning. We'll have to try Payne later."

Joe volunteered to drive back to St. Augustine. He had noticed how the past few days had seemed to wear Anita down, and he suggested she get some rest. She sat in the back, lost in thought. It was almost midnight when they reached their motel, and they went straight to their rooms.

The next morning they woke up before sunrise and drove to the dive shop. Gwen handed them the morning paper when they walked in. "Congratulations," she told them. "You're famous."

The front page had a picture of the little boy they had rescued, standing next to his mother. The headline read "Unknown Heroes Rescue Boy from Alligator."

Frank rolled his eyes. "Good thing we ran when we did."

Joe wore a dreamy expression. "I don't know.

This could be my big break. Maybe they'll hold a parade in my honor and the mayor will give me the key to the city. Not to mention the opportunities for TV endorsements, talk shows . . ."

Gwen shoved two air tanks into his arms. "Get over it," she said with a grin. "We've got a boat to load."

As they sailed toward the site, Gwen briefed them on the fundamentals of finding a sunken ship. "It usually takes years, as your grandfather learned the hard way. First you research the eyewitness accounts, fishermen's records—whatever you can find. The shipwreck was likely to have been a shipping hazard when it first went down, before it broke apart, so you have to look at the historical records.

"If you can narrow the area down to a few square miles, then you can do a grid search, sweeping back and forth until you find it. There are instruments that can help—sonar, magnetometers, depth finders—but none of them are foolproof."

"If my grandfather and Sculley found the wreck, they'd have dropped a buoy to mark the location," Anita said.

"Right," Gwen said with a nod. "If we can get to the right area, we should be able to find the buoy—but even that could take a while."

Gwen picked up an instrument that looked to Frank like a cross between a telescope and a protractor, and raised it to her eye. "Before I used LORAN radio signals, I used to use this sextant to record my dive locations, including Skeleton Key Rock. It's pretty old-fashioned, but it works."

"How does it work?" Frank asked.

"It uses a three-armed protractor to measure two adjacent angles," Gwen explained. "You pick three points on shore, draw a line to each of them, and record the angles to mark the point where the lines meet."

After taking sextant readings, they made several readings using a depth finder mounted on the bottom of the boat before Gwen dropped a marker buoy.

"We'll start our search here. If we've done our homework right, there should be another buoy nearby marking the location of the submarine."

"I don't get it," Joe said. "If you've dived here many times, why didn't you find the submarine before?"

Anita shrugged. "It's not the kind of thing you just bump into, unless you're looking for it. Right now we're about fifteen miles south of where Grandpa thought the wreck would be."

"It's easy to miss things when you're underwater," Frank added. "I read a story about a treasure hunter who found a Spanish ship that sank with millions in gold. He found a modern diver's spear less than fifty feet away from the wreck. Somebody had swum right past without seeing it."

As Gwen had warned, the grid search was tedious. They dropped several more buoys to orient themselves and then made a series of parallel sweeps. Although they hoped to find a buoy left by Mann to mark the location, they also continued to take readings with the depth finder.

It was early afternoon and the clouds were thickening overhead when Anita called out from the upper deck. "Over there—I see it!"

Frank and Joe excitedly dropped anchor as Gwen took sextant readings and recorded the LORAN number for the exact location of the buoy. Frank sensed that they were about to close in on the key to the mystery at last. Would they find the submarine in the depths beneath? he wondered. What would be inside?

Joe had a hard time listening to Gwen as he assembled his diving equipment.

"This dive won't be easy," she said. "We're going down to 130 feet, which means we'll have to make decompression stops and your air won't last nearly as long. Also, you'll have to watch out for nitrogen narcosis."

"Nitrogen what?" Joe asked.

"On deep dives, the concentrated nitrogen you breathe can have a funny, intoxicating effect," Gwen said. "Some divers become disoriented, or lose their judgment and make rash decisions—sometimes with dangerous results."

"That would be so unlike Joe," Anita teased. "To lose his judgment and make a rash decision."

"We'll have to watch out for one another," Gwen said. "Finally, remember that if anybody goes inside the wreck, the stakes go up dramatically."

They continued suiting up in silence. Even Joe knew that Gwen was right. Deep dives were much more dangerous because you couldn't just surface in an emergency. You had to make decompression stops along the way to allow the balance of nitrogen in your blood to adjust.

"We'll hang an emergency air tank to the anchor line," Gwen said. "If anyone is running low on air when we get to the decompression stop, they can breathe off that."

Joe and Anita descended first, followed by Frank and Gwen. They used their hands to pull themselves down the anchor line, fighting the current. The water grew much colder as they went deeper, and Frank was glad to be wearing a wet suit.

As they reached the bottom, Frank couldn't help but be struck by the eeriness of the scene. The water was a dull blue overhead, but along the bottom the horizon faded into darkness.

The mass of something large stretched across the bottom before them. At first Frank didn't recognize what it was because it was half-buried in the sand and almost upside down.

About fifty feet away, covered with coral and barnacles, was the massive hulk of a World War II–era submarine.

Joe couldn't help thinking that they were swimming toward a giant steel coffin as he and Anita led the way toward the submarine. The first part they came to was the conning tower that ordinarily rose upward from the center of the main deck. It had broken apart from the hull as the ship crumbled apart and now lay on its side, covered with weeds and algae.

Swimming closer, Joe cleared away the plant growth and shone his torch on the number "9." Anita looked at Joe, a question in her eyes. As they continued clearing away the algae, his suspicion was confirmed. They had found the wrong submarine. This wasn't U-317, it was U-599!

Frank and Gwen joined them. For a moment they all hovered, stunned. The silence of the ocean amplified the sound of their breathing as the realization hit.

Frank was the first to snap out of it. He and Gwen started swimming toward the bow. Regardless of what submarine they had found, he was determined to explore it.

After about thirty feet they came to a large rupture in the hull of the submarine. The darkness swallowed up the beam from his light as he shone it inside. Frank wasn't claustrophobic, but suddenly he was reluctant to go in.

All the same, his curiosity beckoned him inside, and he could see that, in spite of all her warnings, Gwen was thinking the same thing. She handed him a rope, and he wedged the end of the rope securely in a crack in the outer hull.

Going feet first, Frank half-crawled, half-slipped his way into the submarine. Gwen followed. Inside, it was even more claustrophobic than Frank had imagined. Like a tomb, he couldn't help thinking, but full of barnacles, fish, and who knew what else.

He had heard too many horror stories about divers becoming disoriented and being trapped in wrecks, sometimes only a few feet from safety. His every movement would kick up silt that could make it impossible to see more than a few feet. Even with the rope, they would have to be very careful not to become separated or lost.

They moved by pulling with their arms rather than kicking to avoid stirring up silt. After they had gone about fifteen feet they stopped to get their bearings. Frank had already lost his sense of direction. As he swept his light in a wide arc around him, all he could see was black metal and algae.

Then he froze as he pointed the beam back in the direction they had come. Something gleamed in the beam right next to the opening where they had come in. He recognized ribs, then teeth, then the sunken pits that had once been eyes. The tattered remnants of a uniform still covered the ribs.

It was a human skeleton.

Gwen gripped his arm, her eyes wide. A thrill of fear welled in Frank, too, as he realized they had to swim past the skeleton to get out.

Then he saw something move in the shadows. A chill ran up his spine as a black-suited diver appeared, blocking their exit. Frank and Gwen froze, their hearts pounding as the diver raised a speargun and pointed it directly at them.

For a horrible moment, nobody moved. Frank and Gwen didn't want to startle the other diver, knowing that any mistake might get them killed.

The black-suited diver also seemed unsure of what to do. Still pointing the speargun, he backed toward the exit. But he wasn't looking where he was going. Without realizing it, Frank could see, he was about to back into the skeleton.

The skeleton seemed to reach out to embrace the diver as he bumped into it. A bony hand floated in front of his mask.

The diver jerked his arm wildly up to free himself. In his panic, he squeezed the trigger— and sent a deadly spear right at Frank.

Chapter

11

THE DEADLY SPEAR SPED through the water, straight at Frank. He thought that in another instant it would all be over.

The spear shot past him, missing his ear by inches and puncturing his air regulator hose. The water clouded with bubbles as the air gushed out of his tank, kicking up silt all around them.

Frank's lungs screamed for air. He sucked desperately on the air regulator in his mouth, trying to eke out a few more breaths. As the last air drained from his tank, the world compressed into a narrow, dark, airless space in which he couldn't see or breathe.

He felt a hand grab his shoulder, then somebody—Gwen?—pressed a regulator against his mouth. Grabbing the regulator, he squeezed the purge valve to clear out the water and sucked greedily for several seconds before remembering to control his breathing.

He inhaled deeply one more time and handed the regulator back to Gwen, holding his breath while she took her turn. Frank was glad that he had practiced this technique—known as buddy breathing—so many times.

They passed the regulator back and forth for several moments, looking around for the diver with the speargun, but they could barely see anything because of all the silt. Only by following the life rope did they find their way out.

Several minutes later they emerged from the submarine. Frank felt a huge sense of relief to be out in the open ocean, with blue light overhead.

But they were still 130 feet down. They couldn't surface immediately without risking decompression sickness. Now that Gwen's air tank had to supply them both, it wouldn't last long enough to get them to the surface—or even to the decompression stop, where the emergency bottle was waiting.

Frank saw Joe and Anita a short distance away, clearly unaware that anything had happened. Still passing Gwen's regulator back and forth, Frank and Gwen swam over to join them.

Frank now began breathing off Joe's tank rather than Gwen's. It was a long, slow ascent, but by pooling their air, they had enough to make it to their first decompression stop, where the emergency tank waited.

Joe thought the decompression stop would take forever. The four of them clung to the anchor rope in what Gwen had called the "cluster hang." They were tired and chilled to the bone despite their wet suits. When they finally reached the surface, they all pulled off their masks with relief, gasping in the fresh, salty air.

"If I ever get my hands on that guy, he'll wish he'd never gone anywhere near the water," Gwen said. Frank didn't say anything, but Joe saw the anger smoldering in his brother's eyes.

Anita was the first to climb back into Gwen's boat. "There he goes! He's getting away!" she called down to them. The others quickly followed her up the ladder and looked where she was pointing. A small boat was sailing away. They could see that it had a blue canopy with red trim.

Gwen grabbed a pair of binoculars and held them up to her eyes. "I recognize that boat," she said. "It belongs to Ted Branson. We'll never catch him."

"We'd better pay Branson a visit," Frank said as they started toward shore themselves.

"All this fuss and it turns out we've found

U-599 rather than U-317," Joe said. "Everybody is going to be in for a big disappointment when they find out."

"The only submarine that sank off St. Augustine was U-317," Anita objected. "You guys saw the story in the newspaper."

Gwen nodded in agreement.

"Then how do you explain the fact that U-599 was painted on the conning tower?" Joe asked.

"Either there's more than one submarine, or the submarine that went down in June 1944 wasn't really U-317," Frank said. "One way or the other, we'll find out," he added.

By the time they got back to town and unloaded the boat, it was after dark.

Frank was still determined to talk to Ted Branson immediately, even though his shop would be closed by now.

"Let's go to his house," Frank said. "I want to know who was on that boat, and why we were being followed. It's time for some answers."

They found Branson's address in the phone book. He lived in a large house east of the old town. To get there they had to cross an ornate, arching bridge, called the Bridge of Lions, that linked downtown St. Augustine to the mainland.

Ted Branson looked annoyed as he pulled open the door. "What do you three want?"

Frank held out his punctured regulator hose. "We thought maybe you could explain this."

"What's that supposed to mean?" Branson demanded.

"Somebody tried to shoot me with a speargun this afternoon," Frank said angrily. "That's how this hose got punctured. Whoever it was, they were using one of your boats."

Branson let out a deep breath. "I'm afraid it's probably my son, Dennis, you're looking for. You'd better come inside." He held the door open for them.

"Dennis is missing, and he may have gotten himself into trouble," Branson said. "This morning he took off with one of my boats, without my permission. One of my employees saw him sail away. He hasn't come back, and I'm worried."

"Does the boat have a blue canopy?" Frank asked.

"That sounds like the one." Branson nodded sadly. "It was probably Dennis who stole the equipment that I accused your grandfather of stealing," he said to Anita.

"I don't get it," Joe said. "How can he steal from you? He's your son."

Branson looked down at the floor. "He knew that if he'd asked to use the equipment, I would have refused. Perhaps I've been too strict.

"After Dennis almost died in the accident last year, I forbade him to do any more treasure hunting. I hoped he would find other hobbies, but instead he seemed to lose interest in absolutely everything."

Branson turned to Anita. "When your grandfather showed up the other day saying he'd found U-317, all I thought was, here we go again. I didn't want Dennis involved. That's why I refused to talk to your grandfather. But I was wrong to accuse him of stealing."

"I was wrong about you, too," Anita answered. "I thought you'd set up Grandpa and framed him so that you could keep the gold for yourself."

"If we find out anything about Dennis, we'll let you know at once," Frank promised as they left.

"It sounds like Dennis is the one who shot at you," Joe said once they were back in the Jeep. "Do you think he's mixed up with Demas and his gang?"

"I don't think so," Frank said. "He was alone today. I think he was as scared as we were, and I don't think he meant to pull the trigger."

"So Demas is our only real suspect," Anita said. "How do we find him again?"

"We may not have to," Frank said. "He may find us. Demas and his gang want the submarine—and we know where it is."

"But which submarine?" Joe asked. "U-317 or U-599?"

"I'm not sure," Frank admitted. "Also, I wish

I knew who Demas works for. Remember Sculley's story? He said that when he first met Demas, there was somebody else who stayed in the car."

"Too many questions," Joe said, seeing that Frank's mind was kicking into overdrive. "I'm so tired that I'm not even hungry. Before I can think, I need to get some sleep."

The next morning they showed up early at Gwen's dive shop. "I don't suppose that computer at the dive shop has a modem," Frank said.

Gwen shrugged. "I think it does. I've never used it, though."

"Let me see," Frank said, sitting down. He clicked the mouse several times, then typed a string of codes separated by backslashes. The screen went blank, then ENTER ACCESS CODE was displayed. Frank typed in something else and the words ENTER SEARCH DOMAIN appeared.

"A friend of Dad's showed me this archive," Frank explained. "From here we can search for information on just about any subject, including access to archives that are, shall we say, not always available to the general public."

Joe and Anita watched, hypnotized by the volume of data, as numbers and listings flashed across the monitor. "This is strange," Frank said after a few minutes. "According to the German naval archives, U-599 was sunk in the mid-Atlantic."

Anita looked at the bearings. "That's at least a thousand miles from here."

"Well, they're wrong," Joe said. "The other question is, why does everybody here think that the submarine offshore is U-317, if it really isn't?"

"Because that's what Klaus Krueger told them," Frank answered, remembering the newspaper accounts they had read. "Krueger was the only survivor from the submarine—and it was his testimony that identified the sub as U-317."

"Why would Krueger lie?" Anita asked.

Before Frank could answer, the phone rang. Gwen sounded surprised as she picked it up. "Hello, Mr. Branson. I see. No, we haven't seen him."

She put her hand on the receiver. "It's Ted Branson. He wants to know if we've ever heard of a place called the Sandy Beach Motel."

Gwen listened for several minutes, then hung up. "Somebody spotted Branson's missing boat at a place called the Sandy Beach Motel," she explained. "Ted said he went down there, but he didn't find any sign of the boat or Dennis. He's really worried now."

"Where's the Sandy Beach Motel?" Joe asked.

Gwen looked up the address in the phone book. "It's on U.S. Route 1, about ten miles south of here."

Joe looked at Frank. "Let's head down there."

Anita wanted to go, too, but Joe talked her out of it. "Some things Frank and I do best as a team," he explained.

"If we don't come back, we need you to call the police," Frank added.

"I get it." Anita rolled her eyes. "I suppose boys will be boys. Fine. Chances are you guys will get yourselves in trouble, and Gwen and I will have to come rescue you. Just be careful with the Jeep."

From the dive shop, Frank and Joe drove south out of town on a two-lane road similar to the road north of Vilano Beach. The ocean was on their left but was blocked from view by sand dunes, trees, and homes.

Seeing a sign for the Sandy Beach Motel, they turned left and drove toward the ocean. A minute later they came to the motel.

"Let's not park at the motel," Joe said.

"If we go straight, I think we'll come to the beach," Frank answered. "We can park there."

Soon they came to a large sign:

> BEACH PASS REQUIRED
> ONE WAY, SPEED LIMIT 10 M.P.H.
> NO UNLEASHED DOGS/HORSES
> NO LOUD MUSIC

"Rules everywhere." Joe grinned. "Did we bring our beach pass?"

"It doesn't say anything about parking," Frank answered.

After parking, they walked back to the motel, which consisted of a central building with a lounge and restaurant, surrounded by low bungalows. The place had a run-down, abandoned feeling to it, Frank thought.

But Frank couldn't believe his eyes when he walked into the lounge. Demas was right there, playing a video game!

Frank backed out the door, pulling Joe with him. "It's Demas," he said.

"He'll be so excited to see us—" Joe began.

"Shh!" Frank hissed. "We don't want him to see us, at least not yet." He pointed to a small playground across the street that was partially surrounded by trees. "Let's wait over there. When Demas comes out, we'll see where he goes."

An hour later Demas was still inside, and Joe was getting impatient. "You'd think he would have run out of quarters by now."

Frank gripped Joe's arm. "There he is!" Demas strolled down the path toward one of the more remote bungalows. A four-wheel-drive vehicle was parked in front of the bungalow.

"Let's try to see inside," Frank whispered. Joe followed as he ducked into the trees and made his way around to the back of the cabin. There were two windows on the back wall. Frank crawled up to the first and looked into an empty bedroom. He couldn't see anybody, but he heard voices.

Then he heard somebody cry out in pain. Joe heard it, too. They both ran to the second window. Frank raised his head and took a quick look.

"Dennis Branson is inside, tied to a chair," Frank whispered. "Demas is there, along with Carlos, the guy who tried to nail me with a baseball bat in front of Anita's house."

At the moment he had looked inside, Demas was taking a swing at Dennis. "Oof." Frank and Joe both heard Dennis grunt in pain.

Joe gritted his teeth. "I'm not going to sit and listen to this. There were only two of them, right?"

Frank shrugged. "That's all I could see."

"I'll go around to the front," Joe said. "Give me a minute to get in position, then create a distraction to draw them out."

After Joe ran off, Frank picked up a rock and

counted to thirty. Then he threw the rock as hard as he could through the bedroom window and ran after his brother.

Joe had positioned himself behind a bush on the side of the bungalow. When he heard the crash, he waited. After a moment the door flew open and Demas ran out. Joe charged at him, slamming into Demas's side and bringing him down in a flying tackle.

Then Joe heard a click behind him. "One wrong move, and you die," a voice said.

Joe turned around slowly. Frank was standing a few paces away, his arms up. Carlos stood on the porch, a gun trained on his brother's chest.

Joe had no choice but to surrender. Demas grabbed him roughly from behind and jammed something hard into his lower back, shoving them into the bungalow and forcing them to lie down on the kitchen floor next to Dennis.

"Now we're stuck with three prisoners," Demas grunted. "What a pain. We've already got that other punk to show us where the submarine is. I say we get rid of these two."

Demas chuckled and called out to the Hardys. "Congratulations," he growled. "You two have been looking for the old man. Now you can finally join him—on the bottom of the ocean."

Chapter

12

A CHILL RAN THROUGH JOE as he lay facedown on the kitchen floor. He didn't want to believe it, but Demas's words seemed to mean that Alvin Mann was dead. He thought about Anita—the news would break her heart.

Joe forced himself to focus on the present as Demas pulled a blindfold over his head and tied his hands and feet. If Mann were dead, then he and Frank had to avoid sharing the same fate.

Demas and Carlos finished tying up the Hardys and then walked out of the kitchen. Dennis, who was tied up next to them, started talking as soon as they were gone. "Guys, I'm really sorry about—"

"Shh!" Frank hissed. Demas and Carlos were

talking in the next room, and he was trying to hear their conversation.

"We're not getting rid of these guys until we talk to Stachel," Carlos said. "He wants to keep a low profile for this whole operation, and we don't want him angry at us. Stachel is ugly enough when he's not angry," he added, a quaver in his voice.

"I'm tired of taking orders from Stachel," Demas said. "He acts like he thinks he's still a general or something. Somebody should tell him the war's over, and his country lost. And the same goes for Fritz."

"You shut up," Carlos said. "You want to take on Stachel, you do it on your own. He's a tough old man, even if he is in a wheelchair now."

"I don't care," Demas snapped. "If I have to listen to the story one more time of how he survived the submarine wreck and escaped from that hospital, I'm gonna throw up."

"Okay, okay," Carlos said. "I'm going outside to look around. Those two guys didn't fly here. I want to know how they got here and make sure they came alone.

"Don't do anything with the prisoners while I'm gone," Carlos added. "We might need them, especially if the other kid is lying about knowing where the submarine is."

A moment later Frank heard the door slam

as Carlos went out. They were alone with Demas. He struggled to free his hands, thinking this might be their chance to escape. Next to him, Joe did the same thing.

But they both froze when they heard Demas's voice right behind them. "Don't try anything stupid," the man said. "Or I might have to finish you off now, no matter what Carlos says."

After that they had no choice but to lay still. Joe guessed that a half hour had passed when he heard Carlos return.

"I found their Jeep parked on the beach," Carlos announced. "The registration was in the glove compartment. It belongs to Mann's granddaughter. I also found a card from some dive shop in town called Groves's Aquatic."

These last words chilled Joe's heart. He hoped Anita and Gwen had called the police by now, since Frank and Joe had been gone quite a while.

The two men came back into the kitchen and dragged the Hardys to their feet. "All right, you three, move it." Still blindfolded, the Hardys and Dennis were marched out of the cabin and into the vehicle parked outside. They were in the car for about ten minutes before the engine was turned off again.

"Get out," Demas told them. The smell of fish and the sound of water lapping against boat hulls told Frank they were near water. He was led up a swaying gangplank onto a large boat. The deck felt solid under his feet, barely rocking in the surf.

"Duck your heads," Demas ordered. They went down a stairway and made several turns. When he finally removed the blindfolds, they were in a windowless storage room, empty except for an air compressor and a bunch of scuba tanks. The only light came from a lone bulb over the door.

"Lie facedown on the floor," Demas ordered.

"If you don't mind, I'd rather sit," Joe said.

His answer was a kick in the side. Demas snapped off the light and shut the door, leaving them in total darkness.

Dennis spoke up as soon as he was gone. "You guys aren't going to hurt me, are you?"

"If you haven't noticed, we're tied up, hand and foot," Joe answered. "Not to mention that we're trapped in a dark room, held prisoner by a bunch of psychos who plan to kill us as soon as their ex-Nazi boss gives them permission. So, really, hurting you is pretty low on our list of priorities."

"I've messed things up pretty good for all of us," Dennis went on. "I almost killed you with my speargun—even though I didn't mean to pull that trigger—plus I spilled the beans to Demas and his buddies about finding the submarine."

"You make a pretty strong case for our hurting you," Joe admitted.

"I let my father down, too," Dennis said. "I took his boat without asking. I wanted to find the submarine and make him rich, so he'd be proud of me. Instead, I messed things up for everyone."

After that they fell silent. Time barely seemed to ooze forward as they lay in the darkness. Joe thought about Anita and Gwen. Had they gone to the police yet, or were they still waiting at the dive shop, where Demas and Carlos could show up at any minute? He wished he could warn them of the danger.

After what seemed like hours, Frank felt the hum of the engine vibrating through the floor and realized the boat was moving.

The door opened again, and Demas and Carlos came in. "Stachel wants to see you three on deck."

A few minutes later the Hardys and Dennis stood on deck facing Demas and Carlos, who covered them with automatic rifles. An angular, blond-haired man whom the others addressed as Fritz stood behind them.

The boat they were on was about fifty feet long, with two decks and a fixed diving platform in the rear for divers to get in and out of the water.

Frank scanned the horizon for landmarks.

The Florida coastline was pretty flat, but he guessed they were near the spot where they had located the submarine wreck the day before.

The air didn't feel that much fresher than it had below—hot and damp, with no wind, and overcast. Frank wasn't an expert, but it felt to him as if a storm was heading in.

Fritz spoke up, still standing behind Demas and Carlos. "Thanks to our friend Dennis, we already know that the submarine is somewhere near here." He smiled. "Now we need the exact location."

He looked at Frank, Joe, and Dennis in turn. "Which one of you is going to tell us?"

"First tell us what happened to Alvin Mann," Joe demanded.

"Alvin Mann is dead," said a cold voice behind them. A motorized wheelchair rolled into view, its small engine whirring in the abrupt silence caused by the entrance of this new figure.

Dennis gasped, but Frank and Joe showed no emotion as they stared back at the occupant of the wheelchair. The skin on his face and hands was lined, covered with scars, the lips misshapen, the eyes hard and round, with hairless scabs where the eyebrows should have been.

"You have a great deal of self-control," the man in the wheelchair said to the Hardys after a pause. He spoke with a German accent. "I rarely show my face in public, because most people find it offensive. Considering this is your first time, you handled it rather well."

Frank stared back at him. "Klaus Krueger, I presume."

"Very good." The man in the wheelchair smiled. "Yes, that was the name I used when they pulled me from the ocean."

"His real name is Klaus Stachel," Fritz added.

"Why bother with the fake name?" Joe asked.

Stachel looked offended. "Klaus Krueger was a real name and a real person. It just didn't happen to be *my* name. I borrowed it from him after I killed him. Klaus Stachel needed to disappear. He had a history that would have been misunderstood by many people."

"In other words, he was a war criminal," Frank guessed. "And still is."

Stachel's lashless eyes blazed. "He was a patriot fighting for world mastery. He was strong. Not like the weak Americans who plucked me out of the sea and left me alone in a hospital bed, presuming me to be already dead."

"The records at Menendez Hospital say that you *are* dead," Joe said. "How did you pull that off?"

Stachel steered his wheelchair closer to Joe. "I had nothing to do with that. That foolish hospital orderly, Waldo Payne, did it to cover his own mistake. Payne was on duty that night, but he fell asleep, permitting me to escape. I don't know how he managed to fake the death certificate—or what he used for a body."

Stachel sneered as he went on. "I did some research on Payne and learned that he had a heart condition that kept him out of the military. He must have been very ashamed."

"He shouldn't have been," Frank said. "Having a medical condition is no disgrace."

Stachel looked at him with contempt. "Your modern ideals are very noble. But in 1944, for a young man to be working in a hospital rather than fighting for his country, that was a disgrace. And to have his failure written up in the newspaper, so that the world knew, would have been intolerable."

"I think it's a sad story," Joe said.

Stachel scowled. "Feel sad for yourselves. Unless Payne's weakened heart caves in within the next few hours, he will outlive you."

"Why did Mann have to die?" Frank asked.

"The idiot pulled a gun on me, so I had to shoot him," Demas grunted.

"Mr. Demas didn't actually shoot him," Fritz added, a touch of scorn in his voice. "He tried to shoot him but missed. The bullet hit the gas tank and set off an explosion that killed Mann and sank his boat. Demas nearly died as well, but luckily for him we were following close behind."

"Mann would have had to die in any case," Stachel admitted, "but not until he told us the location of the wreck. Which is why you're going to have to tell us, right now."

"Why should we tell you anything if you're going to kill us anyway?" Frank asked.

"There are good and bad ways to die," Stachel said coldly. "I've seen men beg for death as a form of mercy."

"Even if you kill us, you'll never get away with it," Joe said, trying to sound more confident than he felt. "By now the police should be looking for us."

"Oh, really." Fritz smiled at him. "And who will have called them? Not your pretty little girlfriend."

"Bring the girl on deck," Stachel snapped. Demas disappeared and reappeared a moment later, dragging Anita behind him.

"Anita!" Joe exclaimed. "Have they hurt you?" She shot him a quick look, scared but defiant, as Demas dragged her to the gunwale at the side of the deck and held a knife at her throat.

Stachel turned back to Frank and Joe. "Unless you want us to throw this sweet young girl to the sharks, I'm confident that one of you will show us exactly where the submarine is."

Chapter

13

"HOLD IT!" FRANK'S MIND RACED to think of a way out of their predicament. He didn't mind telling them the location of the submarine, but what then? Once Stachel and his crew knew the location of the submarine, they would have no reason to keep any of them alive, and he would have no more hope of stalling for time.

But if they didn't show Stachel the submarine right now, Demas would cut Anita's throat and throw her to the sharks.

"You win," Frank said finally. "I'll show you exactly where the submarine is. But first tell me which submarine you're looking for."

"Which one do you think?" Demas snarled, still holding the knife against Anita's throat.

"Gee, any submarine will do fine," he said sarcastically. "How many do you know about?"

"I only know about one," Frank said evenly. "But it's U-599. The funny thing is, all the history books say it should be U-317."

Stachel gave Frank a look almost of admiration. "Very well. I will explain. In May of 1944, U-599 sailed from Germany. I was its captain."

"I thought you were the first officer," Joe said.

"Don't interrupt," Stachel snapped. "Klaus *Krueger* was first officer, but of a different boat. I, Klaus Stachel, was the captain of U-599.

"We sailed without authorization of the German High Command. By that time Germany had lost the war, and the High Command had been taken over by traitorous cowards.

"Our crew were still patriots," Stachel continued. "Unfortunately many of us had histories that would have been unacceptable to the victorious allies. So we loaded up the submarine with gold, the product of our conquests."

"You were war criminals, running with stolen booty," Joe said with disgust. "And now you want to recover your gold. All this talk of patriotism, and all you really want is money."

Stachel's eyes blazed. "I'm not interested simply in money. My purposes are much higher."

Demas didn't like the sound of that. "Speak for yourself. I'm in this for money."

123

"You haven't finished the story," Frank prompted Stachel. "How did U-317 get involved, and how did the submarine end up sunk off St. Augustine?"

Stachel nodded. "As I said, the German High Command had been taken over by traitors. When they learned of how we had fled, they issued orders to our own fleet to sink us. The captain of U-317 tried to follow that order by engaging us in the mid-Atlantic. The fool! He could have joined us, but instead we were forced to sink him."

"You turned on your own countrymen," Joe scoffed. "Some patriot."

Stachel ignored him. "After we sank U-317, I realized that it offered a perfect opportunity to cover our tracks. Posing as U-317, we radioed back to Germany that we had sunk U-599. In effect we became U-317. I personally became Klaus Krueger, first officer. Krueger was one of the few survivors from U-317, so I was able to claim his papers to complete my new identity.

"It would have been a perfect escape," Stachel finished, "except that a storm drove us too close to shore, where we were spotted by the Americans."

"What happened to the real Klaus Krueger?" Joe asked.

"We gave him a choice," Stachel said simply. "Join us or die. He chose to die."

"Did you give my grandfather a choice?" Anita asked.

"I'm afraid not," Stachel answered. "He had to die, because we couldn't trust him to keep his mouth shut. But if he had shown us the submarine before he died, nobody else would have had to die. Instead he sent you the journal—forcing us to come after you."

"Can I see his journal?" Anita said, emotion filling her voice.

Stachel shook his head. "I'm afraid there's no time. The journal was useless to us. It only said that the submarine was located near Skeleton Key Rock. But we couldn't find where that was."

"One more question," Frank said, still stalling for time. "If this submarine is so important to you, why did you wait so many years to come after it?"

Stachel's eyes narrowed. "Suffice it to say that I fell out of favor with a certain Latin American ruler."

"Detained." Demas snorted. "In other words, he was stuck in a South American prison. Look, this is all very interesting, but can we get to the point? Time is running short, and the weather doesn't look good."

Stachel glared at Demas, then turned back to

the Hardys. "Now that I've answered all your questions, I trust you'll answer mine. Where is the wreck?"

They were out of time at last. Frank had no choice but to give Fritz the coordinates that they had recorded for the wreck site the day before.

Forty-five minutes later they had found the buoy that marked the submarine and dropped anchor. While the others waited impatiently, Demas and Carlos strapped scuba tanks on their backs and dove down to confirm that the wreck was there. The Hardys, Dennis, and Anita sat helplessly on deck, their hands still tied behind their backs.

The sun was low in the sky by the time the divers returned from their dive to declare that they had found the submarine. Stachel and Fritz were elated, but Demas was less optimistic.

"Recovering the gold isn't going to be easy," he warned. "The hull is almost upside down, half buried in sand. If the gold is stored under the lower decks like you say, salvaging it could take weeks."

"We don't have that much time," Fritz said. "You have to do it faster."

"Salvage diving is dangerous work," Demas said. "Carlos and I aren't going to risk our necks by cutting corners. Not to mention that the weather's looking bad. Sooner or later somebody's going to come looking for these prisoners of ours."

"What are you getting at?" Fritz asked menacingly.

"I think we should dump the prisoners and come back later for the gold, after the heat's off," Demas said.

"We're not leaving without the gold," Fritz growled, his fists tightening. "Otherwise, how do I know you won't sneak back on your own and claim it for yourself?"

Demas bristled at Fritz's words. "We need time," he insisted. "We don't even have the proper equipment onboard for a project of this scale. You never bothered to get half the stuff I asked for."

Fritz and Demas faced each other, fists clenched. For a minute it looked to Joe as if there would be a fight.

"We've got explosives," Carlos suggested. "Why don't we just blast the submarine open?"

"That's crazy," Demas retorted. "The explosives we brought are fine for opening hatches, stuff like that. But they wouldn't be powerful enough to blast through the outer hull."

"What if the explosives were detonated inside the submarine?" Fritz asked. "That would concentrate the force. Plus we could improve our chances by taking advantage of the explosives that are already on the submarine."

"Are you suggesting we rig the explosives to the submarine's torpedoes?" Demas asked.

"Why not? The torpedoes might still have some punch left in them."

Demas wasn't convinced. "And how do you propose that we get the explosives into the torpedo room? It's way up at the front, and since the submarine is almost upside down, the torpedo loading hatch is buried in sand. The only way in is through a crack in the hull, near the middle."

"Go in wherever you have to," Fritz persisted.

"You don't understand!" Demas fumed, his voice shrill. "Penetrating a wreck that far takes time, to clear obstacles and make sure the structure is safe. Trying to do it all at once, under these conditions, would be a suicide mission. Even if you managed to get in and plant the explosives, it's a good bet you'd never make it out. No way I'm going to risk my neck on a job like that."

Suddenly an evil smirk appeared on Stachel's face. "My dear Demas, there's no need for you to risk your neck. We've got two volunteers, ready and waiting."

He turned to Frank and Joe. "Congratulations, gentlemen. You've just earned a new lease on life. We have a mission for you. Unfortunately for the two of you, I don't see how you can possibly survive it."

Chapter

14

"You've got to be kidding," Joe said. "Why should we help you?"

Stachel gestured toward Anita and Dennis. "If you succeed, and we manage to recover our property from the submarine, these two will be allowed to live. We'll drop them on shore after we've made our escape."

Anita shook her head. "Don't do it!" she called.

Frank and Joe hesitated, trying to decide whether they could trust Stachel to keep his promise.

"You really don't have any choice," Stachel said calmly. "People like you never have a choice. You always do the heroic thing. That's your weakness. It makes you predictable."

Fritz smiled at them. "You can take encouragement from knowing that your death will be a historic one. You'll be the last casualties of the Second World War."

"Then let me go with them," Anita pleaded.

"I don't think so," Fritz said. "We need you as insurance. Without you in our sights, we can't be sure that our boys here will do the right thing."

"Let *me* go," Dennis Branson volunteered. "I'm no use to you as insurance. Frank and Joe would probably be glad to throw me to the sharks after the mess I've made."

"Very well," Stachel said with satisfaction. "All the better. Three of you have a greater chance of success than two."

"It's getting dark," Joe said, trying to buy time in the hope that Ted Branson or Gwen had called the police by now. "Can't we at least wait until morning?"

"Nice try," Fritz answered, "but inside the submarine, it's always dark. Who cares what time it is?"

"I still don't like this," Demas muttered. "We're going to arm these three with explosives and send them overboard. How do we know they won't use the explosives to sink us, in spite of the girl?"

"As soon as we drop them into the water, we pull up anchor and sail away," Fritz replied.

"After we hear the explosion, we come back and collect the gold."

"These three heroes will have no choice but to do our work for us," Stachel said, nodding. "Their only option would be to drop the explosives and swim away to drown like cowards, knowing their little girlfriend would suffer the same fate. Better to die quickly in an explosion, with a chance of saving the life of their friend."

"How will we set off the explosives?" Frank asked.

"Don't worry about that," Carlos said. "I'll rig them to your air tanks. Our dive computers are programmed to sound an alert when the air is about to run out. The detonator will be wired to the computer so that when the alert sounds—kaboom."

Demas leered at them. "What could be simpler? To set off the bomb, all you have to do is breathe."

Carlos needed time to rig the explosives to the air tanks, so the Hardys and Dennis had a few hours to prepare for the mission.

Frank dreaded going back inside the submarine. He remembered the oppressive darkness, the sense of being trapped, and the total disorientation caused by all the silt and muck that made it impossible to see anything.

To give them more time to reach the torpedo

room, Carlos told them, they would each carry twin air tanks filled with an oxygen-rich mixture called nitrox rather than air. This would reduce the dangerous effects of nitrogen and increase the time they could safely stay down.

Still, Frank realized that Demas's description of this as a suicide mission was pretty accurate. At 130 feet, even the twin tanks wouldn't last much more than an hour, and even if they reached the torpedo room with time to spare, they would have to sacrifice their remaining air to detonate the explosives.

Stachel sketched them a rough diagram of the submarine while they waited. "From the central control room, you'll need to make your way through the forward crew's quarters," he explained. "Bring a crowbar to force the torpedo room hatch, which will probably be sealed."

Frank listened carefully, but he knew that once they were inside the submarine it would be hard to make heads or tails of where they were. To reach their goal, they would have to rely on their compass—and luck.

Shortly after midnight, Carlos had their tanks ready. "The metal casings for the explosives are welded to the bottom of your air tanks," he explained. "Each of you will carry a charge that will explode once your air pressure is down to three hundred pounds per square inch.

"Don't try to separate the explosive from the

tanks," Carlos warned. "They're very sensitive. Any attempt to forcibly remove them from the tanks will cause them to blow."

As they pulled on their tanks, Anita kept a brave face, but Joe could tell that she was on the verge of breaking down. "Good luck," she stammered, at a loss for words. "I—I'm very proud of all of you."

Frank and Joe exchanged a grim look before they lowered themselves into the water. Neither of them felt the need to say anything. This was as desperate a spot as they had ever been in, but they still hadn't given up hope. Dennis Branson also stayed silent, his face suddenly a mask of resolve.

As soon as they had grabbed the marker buoy rope, the boat drew up the anchor and sailed away as promised, leaving them stranded in the dark in the middle of the ocean. They pulled their masks onto their faces, took one last breath of real air, and then descended into the black depths.

Joe had been diving at night before, but never anything like this. Diving a coral reef under a full moon was one thing. Sinking into an endless sea of blackness was quite another. The darkness swallowed the beams from their head lamps. They could have been in outer space, for all he could tell. Aside from the buoy line, they had no way to orient themselves.

They checked their pressure gauges as they reached the bottom. Each of them had started with their tanks filled to 3000 pounds per square inch. Once they hit 300 pounds, they knew, it would all be over.

Frank held out his regulator to Joe and Dennis, offering each of them a breath from his own tank. Joe understood immediately. By sharing the air, they would use up Frank's tank first. It would detonate ahead of the others, leaving them with two tanks they could use to get back to the surface.

Of course, sharing Frank's tank slowed their progress, and they had to make sure that he wasn't still wearing it when it blew. They also would have to make it back to the surface before the remaining tanks got down to 300.

Joe pulled out a compass and pointed in the direction of the submarine. Several minutes later it appeared in front of them. Joe almost swam into it before he realized that it was there, a dark shadow in the surrounding blackness.

Frank now took the lead and swam to the place where he and Gwen had entered the submarine before. He went in feet first, ignoring the skeleton that had frightened Gwen and Dennis on their last dive.

Once inside, they all felt the added danger of becoming trapped or lost inside the confining structure. Frank offered Joe and Dennis another breath, then checked his air pressure: 2300 pounds left. The others still had 2600 pounds.

Joe looked at his compass. The way the submarine was oriented, they would need to travel almost due south to reach the forward torpedo room.

To avoid kicking up silt, they moved by walking with their fingers rather than kicking, stringing a rope behind them to lead the way out, and hoping against hope that they would be able to use it.

As Frank had feared, Stachel's sketch of the floor plan wasn't much help now that they were down here. Everywhere he looked, all he saw was black metal and muck. The fact that the submarine was lying almost upside down made things even more confusing.

Still, Frank guessed they must be halfway through the crew's quarters as he checked his air again. He was down to 1600 pounds. His tanks were half gone, but Joe's and Dennis's tanks each had almost 2200 pounds left.

Every foot they penetrated into the submarine took them closer to their goal—and farther from safety. They shuddered as they passed several more skeletons, then squeezed their way past a large barrel that had fallen into the corridor, slowing them down even more.

There were only 550 pounds left in Frank's tank when they came to a closed hatch. On the other side, they hoped, was the forward torpedo room. The hatch had a round handle that looked like a steering wheel. Joe tried turning it, but it wouldn't budge.

Remembering Stachel's instructions, Frank pulled out the crowbar he had brought. Dennis and Joe grabbed on as well, and the three of them strained as hard as they could.

Finally, the wheel moved a fraction of an inch. Even then it took several minutes, and lots of precious air, to turn the wheel through several complete revolutions. Then Joe grabbed the handle, braced his feet against the wall, and pulled as hard as he could. The hatch swung open. They were in!

Inside, the torpedoes were mounted on a rack in the center of the room, looking ominous. Would they still pack an explosive punch after more than fifty years?

They didn't have time to wonder. Frank's tank was down to only 410 pounds of air, Joe had 1100, and Dennis just over 900. They had reached the crucial point of their mission. They had to find a way to blow open this submarine, exposing the gold, or Anita would die.

And even if they managed to survive the explosion, they would likely die, too, Joe thought grimly. They had used up most of their air getting in. They wouldn't have enough left to get out.

Unless they found a shortcut, Joe thought. He looked longingly at the four torpedo tubes. Each tube was sealed by an outer hatch that opened to the outside. The lower tubes would be buried in sand, he knew, but the upper tubes just might be exposed to open water, if only they could force the hatch open.

Suddenly Joe knew what to do. It was a desperate plan, but it just might work. And as far as he could tell, it was their only hope of staying alive.

Chapter

15

SUDDENLY FULL OF PURPOSE, Joe swam to Frank and stuffed his own regulator in his brother's mouth. Holding his breath, Joe reached behind his brother and cranked shut the knob on the manifold to completely cut off his brother's air supply.

Frank's eyes widened as he realized what his brother was thinking. Alternately breathing off Joe's and Dennis's regulators, Frank removed his tanks completely, still attached to his BC jacket, and handed the whole apparatus to Joe.

Joe directed Frank and Dennis to leave the torpedo room, and then carried Frank's nearly empty tank to the torpedo tube. The pressure in the two tanks was 390 pounds per square inch—only 90 pounds away from detonating the explosives.

His heart pounding, Joe unscrewed the regulator from the manifold and dropped it on the ground.

Once again he seized the manifold knob that controlled the air supply, ready to open the valve.

He'd have to get this exactly right, or he'd be dead. If he turned the knob too far—allowing the air to rush out too fast—he wouldn't have time to get out of the torpedo room before the air pressure drained down to 300 pounds, setting off the explosion.

Joe turned the knob a fraction of a turn and waited. Nothing happened.

He turned the knob another fraction of a turn.

A stream of bubbles appeared.

Joe didn't know how long it would take for the air pressure to drain down to 300 psi, and he didn't wait around to find out. He turned and swam as fast as he could to join Frank and Dennis. Frank slammed the hatch shut behind him the instant he swam out of the torpedo room.

They braced themselves, shielding their eyes and ears with their arms. Frank had time to wonder how big the explosion would be. If the torpedoes blew, he knew they'd have no hope of surviving.

When it came, Frank thought the crash would split his eardrums. He couldn't believe how loud it was. From outside it might not have been that loud, but here, inside the hull of the submarine, it was like listening to a rock concert from inside a speaker. He gripped his ears, wondering whether any of them would ever hear again.

Still, they were alive. The torpedo room hatch had protected them from the blast. Opening the hatch again, they swam back inside the torpedo room.

Where the sealed torpedo tube had been, the explosion had blown an opening in the outer hull that was large enough for them to swim through. The explosion had made a mess of what remained of the torpedo room, knocking most of the torpedoes off their racks, but none had detonated.

Losing no time, they swam through the opening to the open ocean, emerging from the submarine like human torpedoes.

They still weren't out of danger. Joe's air was down to 960 pounds, and Dennis's was even lower. If they surfaced too quickly, they still risked decompression sickness.

Clinging together, they ascended as slowly as they could, giving themselves as much time as possible to decompress as they shared their remaining air.

They were still sixty feet from the surface when Dennis's tank reached 330 pounds per square inch. Frank quickly shut off the air supply to keep the tank from exploding.

Now they were down to one tank. They ascended another twenty feet before that, too, hit the critical point. Joe gave Dennis and Frank one last breath each, then took one himself as Frank turned off the air on their last tank.

With no air left, they kicked their way upward to the surface, their heads popping out of the water as they sucked in fresh air under the open sky.

For a moment they sat laughing, bobbing in the water, unable to believe they'd made it up alive, then grew quiet once again as the reality of their situation hit. They were stuck in the open ocean, and Anita was still the prisoner of a band of criminals who would be back any minute to claim their gold.

Still, a grim smile grew on Joe's face as he remembered the tank that was still strapped to his shoulders. Suddenly he was filled with deadly purpose. Not only had they made it back from their suicide mission alive, they had brought back a pair of time bombs as well.

Frank, Joe, and Dennis clung to the buoy that still floated above the submarine. The lights from Stachel's boat were visible on the horizon.

Looking up at the sky, Joe realized that he couldn't see any stars. The wind had died, but the sky was overcast.

"You guys should dump those bombs you're wearing, and fast," Frank said. "If anything happens to set one of them off, we're all dead."

"I thought we could use them to sink Stachel's boat," Dennis suggested.

Frank looked at Joe, trying to decide whether Dennis was serious. He had showed great courage under the water, but now that they were back on the surface, Frank was afraid he might return to his old ways.

"Sinking Stachel's boat is a great idea," Frank said, "except then we'd all drown."

Joe knew Frank was right, but he also didn't want to shed the explosives. In the deadly game they'd been forced into playing, they needed a weapon to stay alive. A bomb—used wisely— might save their lives.

"I've got a long rope," he suggested. "We can use it to hang the bombs—uh, tanks—from the buoy. The tanks will hang at a safe distance, and we can pull them up if we need them."

"Good idea," Frank agreed, looking at the horizon. "Looks like our friends are coming back."

"So, what's your brilliant plan?" Dennis asked.

"Sneak aboard," Frank answered. "And then make something up."

When the boat finally closed, it circled several times, apparently searching the water for wreckage or survivors. Frank, Joe, and Dennis waited tensely in the water, ducking under and holding their breath when the search lights swept over them.

Finally the boat shut down the engines and dropped anchor. They waited to see if anything else would happen, but nothing did. Lights glowed in the main cabin, but they couldn't see anybody moving on deck.

"They're probably waiting for sunrise," Frank said. "This is as good a time as any to make our move." Joe and Dennis followed as he swam to the platform mounted to the rear of the boat.

Frank pulled himself up onto the platform and peered over the gunwale. He expected to find himself staring at the barrel of a gun, but the rear deck was empty.

Frank crawled over the gunwale and dropped to his knees behind a large plastic bin used to store diving equipment, thinking that somehow this was all too easy.

Joe was thinking the same thing, but where Frank went, he followed.

"Wait here," he told Dennis.

"And do what?" Dennis asked. But Joe was

already crawling after his brother across the rear deck, toward the cabin. The door to the cabin was closed, so they crawled around the side, where light streamed out the windows.

A loud voice came from inside. It was Demas, and he sounded even madder than usual.

"Carlos and I aren't diving until dawn!" Demas snarled. "If the weather report hasn't improved by then, we come back another day. I'm not risking my neck."

"You do what we say!" Frank recognized Stachel's voice.

"You're not with the Führer anymore!" Demas shot back.

Then the Hardys heard a crash. In spite of the risk, they both lifted their heads to look into the cabin. Fritz lay on the floor. Demas stood over him holding a gun. Stachel sat in his wheelchair, his disfigured face now showing fear. Carlos stood back, holding a speargun, apparently not sure which side to take.

Anita was tied up in the corner. Joe saw with relief that she looked unhurt.

"I'm taking over," Demas grunted. "As of now. Now that we know where the gold is, I don't need either of you."

"What do you plan to do with them?" Carlos asked.

"Kill them," Demas said simply. "Except the girl. She might be useful as a hostage."

Demas aimed the gun at Fritz's head. "So long, friend. It's been a pleasure."

Joe was about to do something—he hadn't quite figured out what—when the rear door of the cabin flew open and Dennis Branson stepped in.

Chaos erupted in the cabin. Demas whirled toward Dennis. Fritz jumped up, grabbed the gun from Demas's hands and slammed the butt of the gun into Demas's forehead, knocking him down. Carlos ran toward Dennis, punching him in the stomach and pushing him back through the cabin door.

Joe gritted his teeth. Bullets could start flying any second, and Anita was tied up inside the cabin! He jumped up and ran around the cabin toward the doorway. Before he got there he found himself face-to-face with Fritz.

"You!" Fritz snarled.

Joe grinned at him. "Surprised to see me?"

"I don't know how you survived," Fritz growled, raising the gun. "But you won't live any longer."

Frank appeared around the corner, slamming into Fritz and knocking him toward the gunwale. Fritz tumbled onto the deck. Frank fell on top of him, trying to wrestle the gun out of Fritz's hands.

Fritz struggled to his feet, straining to aim the barrel of the gun toward Frank. Joe charged to help his brother, running right at Fritz.

Fritz ducked to the side, tripping Joe and shoving him toward the gunwale. Unable to stop himself, Joe flew forward, bumping his head against the gunwale, and fell overboard.

"Joe!" Frank called. He forgot Fritz as he saw his brother disappear overboard. He ran to the gunwale and looked over, but all he could see was black water. "Joe!" he called again.

Then Frank felt Fritz's gun pressed against his back. "Forget about him," the man grunted, bringing Frank down with a blow to the back of the head.

Then Frank heard gunshots. Carlos was spraying the water with bullets, right where Joe had gone overboard! Frank struggled to get up, but Fritz brought him down again with another kick, and everything went black.

Joe hit the water with a splash. His head throbbed, but the water woke him, clearing his senses. Expecting a hail of bullets to rain down on him, he took a deep breath, ducked his head under the water, and swam directly under the boat.

When Frank woke, he was tied up in the cabin. Dennis, Anita, and Demas were tied up next to him, and Carlos held the speargun trained on them all.

"Are you all right?" Anita whispered to him.

Frank nodded, even though his head felt like a train wreck. "How about you?" She shrugged.

Stachel and Fritz sat at a table, talking about what to do next. Stachel was still determined not to leave without the treasure. "You and Carlos can still dive for the gold," he said.

"Forget it," Fritz said. "I'm not a trained diver."

"Fritz is right," Carlos said. "This isn't the time. The weather's getting worse."

"If we're leaving the gold here, then all the prisoners must die," Stachel said coldly. "We can't leave behind anybody who knows where it is."

Frank looked at Anita when he heard Stachel's words. She looked back at him, her eyes desperate. His head throbbed, but he had to think. He looked at Demas. Even he could be an ally now.

"If they die, then we all die." Frank recognized the voice, but it sounded strangely distant. Stachel and Fritz heard it, too. Fritz and Carlos whirled, raising their weapons.

Joe Hardy stood in the cabin door, holding a pair of scuba tanks that had been wired with explosives and converted into a time bomb. His hand gripped the knob that he could turn to drain the air out of the tank, setting off the bomb and killing them all.

"Put down your weapons and get down on the floor," Joe said grimly. "Or we all die."

Chapter

16

EVERYONE IN THE ROOM FROZE and stared at Joe in disbelief. His head was reddened from a cut on his forehead, his eyes blank, his face determined.

"Very well," Stachel said finally. From somewhere he produced a small revolver and aimed it directly at the scuba tanks in Joe's hands. "If that's the way you want it, we'll die together. I refused to surrender in 1945, when my country faced defeat, and I'm not going to surrender now."

Next to him, Frank heard Anita suck in her breath. For a moment he realized that he wasn't breathing either. They all sat paralyzed as Stachel and Joe stared into each other's eyes, facing off.

Then Frank recovered his senses. Although his hands and feet were tied, he started to worm his way across the floor toward Stachel's wheelchair. He knew that Fritz and Carlos could see him, but even they said nothing.

Once he was in position behind the wheelchair, he rolled over onto his back and bent his legs. Then he looked back at Anita and mouthed a single word.

She got the message and let out a bloodcurdling scream.

Stachel whirled at the sound for just an instant, but that was all the time Frank needed. He shot his legs forward, knocking over Stachel's chair.

Suddenly the cabin was flooded with light, and a voice blared from a loudspeaker: "This is the police. Come out with your hands up."

Fritz ran across the room and grabbed Anita, but Joe was on him in a second, pulling him off. Demas also tried to struggle to his feet, even though he was tied hand and foot, but Frank kicked out at him, bringing him down again.

A second later several policemen charged into the cabin. "Everybody freeze!" they ordered. Finally defeated, Fritz, Carlos, and Stachel raised their hands above their heads and were taken out of the cabin. Demas was hauled out after them.

Ted Branson and Gwen called out from the

deck of the police boat as the Hardys and their friends filed onto the deck. As soon as they boarded the police boat, Gwen ran up and hugged Anita.

"I was so worried about you! Anita left the dive shop to pick up some lunch and never came back," she explained. "I called the police, then called Ted Branson."

"One of the motel guests had already complained about Demas and Carlos," Branson continued, "so the motel staff led us right away to the bungalow they had rented."

"From there, it wasn't too hard to figure out where we might find you," Gwen explained. "We came as fast as we could."

Gwen smiled at Anita. "Plus, I have the most important news of all to deliver. The Coast Guard picked up your grandfather a few days back, almost fifty miles south of here. He didn't go down with his ship after all! He was almost unconscious when they picked him up. He'd been drifting in a life jacket for days, and for several days they didn't even know who he was. But they say he's going to be all right."

Anita hugged Gwen more tightly, then collapsed sobbing in Gwen's arms. "He's all right," she said over and over. All the emotion she had bottled up in the last days poured out. "I can't believe it, that he's all right after all! Somehow I always knew, but I was so scared."

Then she turned to Frank and Joe. "More than anybody, I have you two to thank."

"It was nothing," Frank started to say.

"It was everything!" she said. Catching Joe's eyes, she gave him a long smile. He smiled back. "Thank you for everything," she said again, her voice barely more than a whisper.

Several days later a happy group sat on the beach north of St. Augustine. Alvin Mann had just been released from the hospital, and was enjoying his first day out. Still sunburned from his ordeal, he had fashioned a tent out of a tarpaulin to shelter himself from the sun, but the Hardys could tell his spirits were high.

"You really should be inside, Grandpa." Anita smiled at him.

"Nonsense," Mann grunted. "Trying to get rid of me already? Nothing like a day on the beach to cleanse the soul. This is all the healing I need."

"You know what the doctors said," Gwen reminded him.

"Doctors!" Mann answered. "I didn't take orders from the band of goons even when they had a gun on my head, and I'm not taking orders from any doctor either."

"One thing I've been wondering," Frank said. "When Demas shot the gas tank, how did you survive the explosion?"

"I wasn't even on the boat when the explosion happened. I jumped off long before it went down. Near as I can figure, Demas caused the explosion so that he could claim I was dead. He didn't want to admit to the others that he'd missed me."

"Have you heard anything else about the gold yet?" Joe asked.

"Most of it will probably go to lawyers," Mann said. "So many people are fighting over it. A couple of Norwegian banks claim they should get it, since it was theirs in the first place. The State of Florida wants in on the action, too. But the total haul will be worth several hundred million. If we get even a small share of it, it will be more than enough for us. More than we've ever dreamed of having. Of course, we want to give you two a nice reward."

"That's not necessary," Joe said. "The adventure is reward enough—that and knowing that all of you are safe."

"That we are." Anita grinned. "And we've got big plans, too. Mr. Groves, the owner of the dive shop, has announced that he's retiring. So Gwen and I are buying the shop together. Gwen can keeping running the diving end of the business, and I can move my film production company underwater. I have ideas for several documentaries, maybe even a feature film."

"A feature film!" Joe exclaimed. "That

sounds great. Maybe Frank and I can take the starring roles!"

"And this time, they *will* get our names for the press," Frank added with a laugh.

"Just one thing," Joe said. "Whose name will go first in the credits?"

"Respect your elders, little brother," Frank said as he took a playful swing at Joe, then chased him down the beach as grandfather and granddaughter looked on, laughing.

HAVE YOU SEEN THE NANCY DREW FILES™ LATELY?